LILLY'S JOURNEY

LILLY'S JOURNEY

Cheryl Anita Lewis

LILLY'S JOURNEY

iUniverse books may be ordered through booksellers or by contacting:

iUniverse
1663 Liberty Drive
Bloomington, IN 47403
www.iuniverse.com
1-800-Authors (1-800-288-4677)

ISBN: 978-1-5320-5089-3 (sc)
ISBN: 978-1-5320-5090-9 (e)

Library of Congress Control Number: 2018906384

Print information available on the last page.

iUniverse rev. date: 07/20/2018

With much love, to my mother and late grandmother,
who inspired me to write this story

CHAPTER 1

∽ ❖❖❖ ∽

MEMORY FADES OVER time, so there's a lot I don't remember about life as a young girl in the backwoods of Georgia in 1949. What I distinctly remember is my cousin Rosalie Baker romping into our lives from the big city of Chicago at the end of June. During her visit, I became aware of the *heartbeat* of life. She had that kind of effect on people.

The heat of the night was hindering me from sleeping, and I couldn't understand why anyone else in the little sharecropper shack where I lived *was* able to sleep. I was stretched out on top of the covers, listening to the crickets and staring up at the ceiling. The dim light of the moon barely illuminated the room through the open window. Sweat ran down my forehead, collected in my armpits, and dampened my back.

Rosalie was lying next to me, sleeping like a baby. I liked my cousin, but I also felt crowded, as there were now four of us sharing the bedroom. My mother, Mamie Lee Brown, and my younger sister, Vivian, were asleep in the other bed.

I was born in Haynesville, Georgia, on August 16, 1939. When I was five, we moved to Buffalo to live with my aunt LaRue. Mama worked cleaning houses for a while, but after she suffered a nervous breakdown, we moved back to Georgia so that her parents could help care for us.

As I lay in bed, I thought back to the previous week when Rosalie had first arrived. I recalled listening to my grandfather saying, "Where you suppose she gone sleep?" My grandfather, Homer Clayborn, had posed that question to Mother, but he didn't wait for an answer. That was a good thing because Mother didn't talk much anymore. My grandmother's name was Eunice Clayborn, but everyone called her "Mother."

"Ain't nowhere for her *to* sleep," Grandpa had continued, answering his own question. "She might as well just stay on where she is. We overcrowded in this here shack, and ain't no room for one more person." Of course, the shack had housed at least six people at one time. But what Grandpa really meant was that he didn't want any more residents, not even on a temporary basis.

I didn't know if it was Mother who had changed Grandpa's mind, but shortly after that conversation, we drove into town to pick Rosalie up from the bus station. She lived with her parents and her older sister, Rhonda. They had moved away several years earlier so my aunt, Eula Mae Baker, and her husband, Willie Earl, could find work. I was four the last time I had seen Rosalie.

My cousin's head was crowned with short curly black hair; her skin was brown; and, when she talked, my attention was always on the beauty mark on her left upper lip. We looked nothing alike, except for the wide nose that was a family trait. I was the lightest person in my family and the only one with reddish-brown hair that, to me at least, felt like sandpaper.

Rosalie was fourteen. And when she came to town, it was like when Mother added too many cayenne peppers to her homegrown collard greens or when the firecrackers went off on the Fourth of July. She was all sass and attitude. When she came to town, my life changed. Or at least my mind did—I began to dream. Rosalie was smart and as bold as a lion. She wasn't even afraid of Grandpa, which I thought was a requirement for everyone who lived in the shack with him.

I used to think Grandpa was the meanest man alive. When he called your name, you could count on hearing your name *plus* a cuss word or two. In retrospect, perhaps he wasn't so mean. Maybe he was just plain tired.

There was no question that he was tired of picking cotton, which had been his occupation since the age of five. When he stood, he sort of leaned forward, and his face and hands looked more like crinkled brown leather than skin from all that time he'd spent out in the sun.

Grandpa never had enough money, and he hated being called "uncle" by the white men he encountered in town. He was probably tired of a lot of other things that I, as a little girl, wasn't aware of.

Grandpa and Mother had raised their children, six of them, and then they found their two-bedroom house full all over again.

When Rosalie first arrived, she was careful to be respectful around her elders. But when she was alone with Vivian and me, she said, "Y'all know I don't want to be here, don't y'all?"

At the time, I thought that was a strange question because how was I supposed to know that she didn't want to come to visit us?

A few days after Rosalie came to Haynesville, she, Vivian, and I took the long walk to town to the post office. Auntie Eula Mae had sent Rosalie a letter containing some money. On the way back home, we saw our friend Thomas Foster. He was working on a farm cutting hay with a tractor. He got off the tractor and met us on the road.

"Hey, ladies," he said.

"Hi, Thomas," replied Vivian.

"Hi, Thomas," I said. "This is our cousin, Rosalie. You remember her? She used to live here, but now she live in Chicago. She visitin' for the summer."

Thomas was a tall, thin boy who seemed to exist on the sheer power of *hope*. He was living his life for the day when he and his family would finally move to Milwaukee and forever escape the drudgery of sharecropping. With a big grin on his face, he said, "I sure do remember you, Rosalie. You sure did grow up to be a pretty girl."

"Boy, I don't know you. Don't be talkin' to me like that."

Thomas's smile was suddenly a frown. "What's wrong with you, girl? I was just payin' you a compliment."

"Well, don't be payin' me no compliments," Rosalie said. She shoved Thomas with such force that he fell backward on his butt. I couldn't believe what Rosalie had just done.

And it got worse. Rosalie jumped on Thomas and started punching him in his chest and face.

I was horrified, confused, and embarrassed. I really couldn't believe what Rosalie was doing. I tried to pull her off Thomas, but I caught her elbow in my chin. The hit was so hard that I thought my teeth were going to shatter. I backed away, screaming for her to get off Thomas.

Vivian was jumping up and down like she was on a trampoline. She was crying and shouting for them to stop it. Poor Thomas didn't defend himself. Instead, he covered his face with his crossed arms.

Grandpa and Uncle Buddy seemed to appear out of nowhere. They pulled up to the scene of the crime in my uncle's rattling green Model T Ford. Uncle Buddy hopped out of the car and yanked Rosalie by the arm. "We came lookin' for y'all 'cause y'all was takin' so long. Now I see why. Get in this here car. All a y'all. *Get in this here car.*" He was angrier than I had ever seen him.

Thomas was on his feet, dusting off his overalls. He was glaring at Rosalie, who had gotten in the car and was sitting between Vivian and me in the back seat, and she was glaring back at him.

"You all right, boy?" Uncle Buddy asked Thomas.

"Yes, sir. I'm all right."

"All right. Get on back to yo' work then. We gone deal with this here girl."

Uncle Buddy, a carpenter who made beautiful furniture, was my grandparent's oldest son. He was a muscular man who looked out for Grandpa and Mother. He also kept an eye on the baby of the family, Uncle Henry, who had served a brief stint in World War II and came back from the war muttering to people whom only he could see.

On the way home, Grandpa gave Rosalie a lecture with a lot of cuss words about not coming down south and acting like a fool. "You a visitor down here. You not gone be comin' down here causin' no whole lotta confusion." And he punished her for her strange behavior.

"When we get home, girl, you get yo' tail in that house and go to bed. And I don't wanna see yo' face until the mornin'. And you gone apologize to that boy. What's wrong with you? You ain't gone be comin' down here actin' a fool."

Rosalie ran into the house and to the bedroom. She had made a terrible mistake getting on Grandpa's bad side so soon after coming to Haynesville. Grandpa and Uncle Buddy didn't take any mess.

I wondered what kind of summer it was going to be.

⸺ ✦✦✦ ⸺

Mama's skin was a smooth brown. Her soft black hair was always worn in a braid and wrapped around her head in a crown. She had a strong body that was well equipped for all the work she had to do. Mama had recovered from her breakdown, and no one ever talked about it. She was standing in our dimly lit little kitchen ironing a dress for one of the white ladies in town. The kitchen had a potbellied stove and one window that we shuttered closed with a little door.

"Mama. Mama. Rosalie jumped on Thomas and beat him up," Vivian said, all excited, in her squeaky little voice.

Mama's eyes were wide as saucers, the whites of her eyes no less white than the cotton in the fields. She sat the iron down on the wooden board that Uncle Buddy had made.

"Vivian, child, what are you talkin' about?"

"*Rosalie beat up Thomas,*" she repeated.

"Well, that don't make no sense to me, little girl. How she beat up Thomas? She don't know Thomas, and Thomas is as big as the sky."

We told Mama exactly what had happened. We told her that Thomas *did* remember Rosalie from when she was a little girl; after all, they were around the same age. They used to play with each other.

We told Mama that Grandpa and Uncle Buddy had come looking for us and how angry they had been and that Grandpa had told Rosalie she had to stay in the bedroom for the rest of the day.

"I told them to go lookin' for y'all. I was gettin' worried because you all was gone too long. Let me go talk to this child," Mama said.

Mama pushed the curtain aside and stepped into the room, my sister and I behind her. I followed Mama into the room because I was nosy and wanted to hear what the teenager had to say for herself.

Rosalie was lying on the bed, staring at the ceiling.

"Rosalie, what's this about you attackin' Thomas?" Mama asked.

Rosalie rolled over, showing us her back. "He made me mad."

"Turn over and look at me, Rosalie," Mama said.

Rosalie turned over, sat up, and hugged her legs, but she didn't look at Mama.

Mama's voice had tenderness but firmness in it. "You see how big and strong Thomas is? He could hurt you."

"I don't think so. *I hurt him.*"

Mama's hands were on her thick hips, and she shook her head. "Rosalie, you as stubborn as that ole mule we got out back, and you got the wrong attitude. You know you got to be in here the rest of the day wit' no supper."

"I don't care. I don't want to eat no sowbelly anyway."

Mama repeated, "You got the wrong attitude. I never seen the beat in my life." Mama often said, "I never seen the beat in my life," when she was perplexed.

I didn't blame Rosalie for not wanting any sowbelly, which was salt pork from the belly of a hog. Sometimes Grandpa would take our dog, Gus, hunting for possum or rabbit, and that would be our meat. But sowbelly made the most frequent appearances on our dinner table.

Rosalie was angry about having to come to Georgia. She told Vivian and me the reason she had to come to stay with us was because her parents were having problems in their marriage. She said that, all of a sudden, her father was being unreasonable. He was saying that because he was light-skinned and Rosalie was brown-skinned, she did not belong to him. Rosalie looked like her mother. And her sister, Rhonda, was light-skinned and favored their father.

"It took him all these years to figure out that I look like Mama and not him." Rosalie's voice contained a mixture of sadness and anger. "Mama tried reasoning with him, but there is no reasoning with him. He started changing after we moved to Chicago. Mama said maybe with some time apart, he would come back to his senses. She said hopefully everything will be back to the way it was before. I hope so because I want to go home and go to school in September."

"Why you think he change like that?" I asked. We were walking in the road, going home from a visit to Uncle Buddy's house. Uncle Buddy's wife, Aunt Pearline, had invited the three of us girls to their house for dinner.

"I don't know," Rosalie replied. "But I sure do wish he would change back to the way he was before. He was nicer then."

I felt bad for Rosalie because of her troubles. What she told us helped me to somewhat understand her bizarre behavior when she first came to Haynesville. At the same time, I envied her for being able to go to school nine months out of the year.

Our school was a one-room class with all grades mixed together. It had seemed to me that I was in the second grade for too long, so one day I decided to promote myself to the third grade. I did so by moving one seat forward.

We only went to school now and then. The walk was long, and many days, by the time we arrived, school was already over. No one had a book, but we knew that wasn't the way it was for the white kids. They had books and were graduating from high school and going to college.

Rosalie told us she was going to go to college. She also said she was going to be in the Olympics.

"Olympics? What's that?" I asked. It sounded so dramatic.

"You know what it is?" she asked Vivian. I don't know why she asked Vivian. She was younger than me. How would she know if I didn't?

My sister shook her head.

Rosalie explained the Olympics to Vivian and me. She told us about Jesse Owens. Facts about Jesse Owens rolled off Rosalie's tongue as if he were a close friend of hers.

"His father was a sharecropper just like Grandpa. And his ancestors were slaves the same as ours. He won four gold medals at the 1936 Olympics in Berlin, Germany."

"Where is Berlin, Germany?" Vivian asked.

"It's far away, in another country. Anyway, I'm going to run track in an all-Negro college."

I gasped. We *were* eating her dust every time we raced, but this sounded unbelievable. The thought of going to college had never entered my nine-year-old mind. But at that moment, I wanted to move back up north. If Rosalie could finish high school, go to college, and do something important with her life, then I could too!

"Mama said she's going to make sure I go to college. She said that if she has to work day and night, every day, I'm goin'. But she said I have to make sure I don't have any babies out of wedlock."

"What's wedlock?" I asked.

Rosalie looked at me. I was beginning to realize how much I annoyed her. "Don't you know anything?" She sighed, sucked her teeth, and shook her head. "Wedlock means marriage. If you have babies out of wedlock, it means you have them before you get married. Mama said God doesn't like that and it can mess up your future. Mama said it's hard enough for Negroes without us sabotaging our own future."

"Your mother's a smart lady," I said. I didn't dare ask her what *sabotage* meant!

CHAPTER 2

—◆◆◆—

OUR DWELLING PLACE was a two-bedroom shack made of plywood, with cold air blowing through the gaps during the winter. A long, wide dining table sat in the dining/living room, the first room that one entered upon stepping into the shack. The next room was the kitchen, which was barely big enough for the wood-burning stove and the person doing the cooking. During the winters, our legs would turn a shade darker as we huddled around the stove trying to keep warm. Skillets, pots, and cooking utensils hung from hooks on the wall.

To the right of the kitchen were the two bedrooms, which were separated by a long, heavy curtain.

Grandpa's barn housed a pig and cow, and we had chickens for eggs and meat. Mother and Mama had a small vegetable garden and made delicious meals and desserts from canning. Uncle Buddy and his family lived down the road from us on the same sprawling property.

Summertime brought a short respite from doing the awful, hard work of picking cotton. At cotton-picking time, Grandpa would always say, "Abraham Linckin done freed the slaves, but we still slaves." My young mind couldn't understand what he meant because, to me, if Abraham Lincoln had said Negroes were free, then we were *free*. But Grandpa wasn't one for questions or explanations.

The cycle of cotton planting began in early February. We harvested the crop from August to late November. As a consequence, we couldn't go to school until after the crop was in. We worked approximately fifty acres of land. Everyone in our household worked the land.

Uncle Buddy and his three young sons and Uncle Henry picked the cotton as well. Uncle Buddy's wife didn't work the fields because she was a maid/nanny in town.

When we went to the cotton patch, each person, including the children, brought a large bag that went over the shoulder. The over-the-shoulder bag left both hands free to pick the cotton. We laid a burlap sack on the ground to dump the cotton in once the sack was full.

The sun was punishing, and Vivian, being the youngest, was especially miserable and spent most of her working time crying to go home. For all our work, we were paid three dollars for each hundred pounds of cotton. Mama and Mother made sunbonnets to protect us from the sun. But we didn't wear gloves. By the end of each day, our hands hurt from being pricked by the cotton bolls.

Mother was a tiny woman; she stood less than five feet tall and probably didn't weigh much more than one hundred pounds. I felt sorry that she was so small and old and had to still be picking cotton.

Rosalie cursed the first time she bled from being stuck by the cotton boll. Grandpa told her he would wash her mouth out with soap if she talked like that again. She only picked cotton for a couple of weeks because she went home in September, but she complained incessantly about being out in the field.

"It's bad enough that I have to come down here and pick cotton like I'm some slave on a plantation. But on top of it, *Grandpa's a hypocrite.*"

"What's a hypocrite?" I asked.

"Grandpa's a hypocrite. He can cuss, but I can't. He's a hypocrite. And he calls himself a preacher! And you need to go to school so you can learn some words!"

I was a sensitive young girl. Rosalie hurt my feelings by that comment, even though what she said was true. *And* she made me nervous. I hoped she wouldn't be crazy enough to try to fight Grandpa the way she'd done with Thomas. That would not have been a fight she would have won.

During cotton-picking season, we worked from sunup to sundown, usually seven days a week. The only exception was when it rained. To this day, I still love the rain.

Thomas had cheerfully said, "You know they makin' machines to pick all this cotton. Soon we won't have to pick no more cotton!"

"Hallelujah," I said.

Then Thomas turned serious. "I'm movin' to Milwaukee soon anyway, so either way, my cotton-pickin' days is almost over."

— ❖❖❖ —

Because our schooling was so sporadic, before Rosalie came to Haynesville, Vivian and I could hardly read, and our math skills were just as poor. The families in the backwoods didn't have too much time for education. We had to work in order to survive, and all hands were required. But after our work was done, and when she was in the mood, Rosalie would spend time teaching us to read from a bunch of magazines that I had found in the woods.

"The schools in Chicago are segregated. Almost everything is. But at least we *go* to school," Rosalie said. When she returned home, she would be going into the eleventh grade at DuSable High School. She said the school was named for a colored man who was the first person to settle in Chicago.

Rosalie said they had electricity where she lived, but we had to do our studying by kerosene lamp. She wasn't the most patient teacher. Sometimes she would suck her teeth and huff. "Come on now, girl," she would say to either of us. "That's an easy word."

We stammered and stumbled, but by the end of Rosalie's visit, we had learned more from her than we ever had from our sporadic times going to school. And I was impressed by her proper manner of speaking. I started imitating her, and I told Vivian to do the same.

I started pestering Mama about moving up north. "Maybe we can move to Chicago with Auntie Eula Mae and her family," I suggested one hot sunny day when I was helping her with laundry. Mama washed our family's laundry outside in a large pot. She also "took in laundry" for some of the white ladies in town.

"Eula Mae got her own troubles," Mama said. "Maybe we can move back to Buffalo with Bessie anem." When Mama said *anem*, she meant "and them."

Mama was the eldest of four sisters. Auntie Eula Mae was a couple of years younger than Mama. LaRue Cox was the sister we had lived with during our time in Buffalo. And the youngest sister was Bessie Williams.

She lived in Buffalo with her husband. All the aunts came home a couple of times per year to check on their parents.

"No, Mama! Aunt Bessie don't even like us," I said to her suggestion about living with Bessie. Bessie definitely *was* mean, and I didn't like her. I loved my other aunts. Eula Mae carried herself like royalty and treated others well. LaRue was stern, but I had no doubt she loved me. Her voice was musical, and even when she talked, she sounded like she was going to break out singing at any moment.

Aunt Bessie had moved to Buffalo with Auntie LaRue, gotten a job in a factory, and eventually married. I couldn't figure out who on God's green earth would marry Aunt Bessie. When she'd lived in Haynesville, her favorite place was the juke joint in the Bottom. Most of the time, she would get drunk and come back acting ugly.

One evening when Aunt Bessie had come back home for a visit, already tipsy, she had gotten dressed to go out. I was sitting on the porch playing with my paper dolls that I had made from my magazines. Her two friends from the Bottom were waiting for her outside in their car. When she was walking down the stairs, her high heel got caught between a gap in the wood, and she went falling down.

I couldn't help but to laugh.

She looked up at me and hopped up like a rabbit. "Girl, what are you laughin' at?" she asked. Her stockings had runs and holes, and she was dusting red clay dirt off her new yellow dress.

"You go get me a switch so I can whoop you," she demanded.

Her friends, who had gotten out of the car to help her up, told her they didn't have time for all of that, but Aunt Bessie was determined to whip my behind.

I regretted laughing at her. What a humiliation it was to have to get the branch from the tree so the adult could whip you, make you cry, and then demand that you stop crying because they were hurting you.

"And hurry up about it," Aunt Bessie hollered as I went out back to get my whipping stick. I handed it to her. She dragged her hand over the stick so that there was no longer any leaves on it. Then right in front of her friends, she grabbed my arm tightly so I couldn't get away and proceeded to cut my legs up with that switch.

I danced around, jumping and crying, hopping on one leg and then the other. I did evade some of the hits, but most of them landed on my skinny legs.

Grandpa, who had been resting, came outside to see what all the commotion was about.

"Bess, why you hittin' on that girl?" Ain't you suppose to be gone somewhere?"

"I'm gone, Daddy," Aunt Bessie said, huffing and puffing. She threw the stick on the ground and got into the car and took off with her friends.

I was glad that Aunt Bessie had moved away and was sorry to see her whenever she came back home for a visit. She was the main one who called my sisters and me, "Joe Brown's seed."

"Girl, why you got them whelps on your legs?" Mama asked me after she had come home from delivering laundry to her customers in town. One of the customers had given her a ride home.

"Aunt Bessie whooped me with the switch," I said. I hoped Mama was going to set her sister straight.

Mama didn't go to the juke joint. She called the music *gutbucket music* and the women were *fast tailed*.

"What's gutbucket music?" I had asked Mama.

"The blues. Everybody got the gutbucket blues."

Mama asked me why Aunt Bessie had used the switch on me.

"Because I laughed at her when she tripped on the steps."

"Well, you know better than to laugh at people, don't you? Especially Bess. You know Bess got the fightin' spirit in her."

"Mama, you gonna tell her not to be whoopin' on me?"

"No. I'm just tellin' you to keep yo' distance. Stay outta her way and don't be sassin' her. She'll be goin' home directly anyway."

I believe my mother was intimidated by, if not afraid of Aunt Bessie. Mama was a gentle, mild-mannered woman who avoided confrontation as much as possible.

Mama said that we were the "black sheep" of the family. She reckoned that was because she had married my daddy, who was thirty years older than she was and not well liked. He'd had another family before he married Mama, and his oldest child was only slightly younger than Mama. And according to the family, Mama was "slow." Mama was the one who needed help, who couldn't seem to make it without her parents.

They also called me "slow" and "awkward." I *was* clumsy and uncoordinated, and I was always falling and scraping my knees. Sometimes I had the feeling of not belonging. I would retreat to the unoccupied bedroom in my downtime and draw thin women with large almond-shaped eyes and eyelashes the length of a whisk broom. Or I'd take long, slow walks down the road with Raggedy Ann, telling her I was going to leave Georgia behind one day and create beautiful dresses for beautiful women in New York.

I believe my sisters stood in a little more favor with the family than I did. Vivian and our older sister, Honey, whose real name was Vera, were beautiful girls. Honey and Vivian both had long wavy black hair and were brown-skinned like Mama. My sisters were more graceful in their movements than I was. Even Vivian, at her young age, had a sort of glide to her walk, as opposed to my clomping style.

When I looked in the mirror, it told me I was kind of funny-looking. Mama said I resembled my father, whom I had never known or even seen a picture of. They said he had long thin hair. According to family, he was "light, bright, and almost white." For some reason, he was called "Ole Mex."

I thought it was unfair that I resembled (and not in a flattering way) a man with whom I would never have one encounter. He was killed one Sunday morning while walking on the railroad tracks. Vivian was a baby when our father died. Mama said that my father had money before the stock market crash, but when he died, he had one quarter in his pocket.

When Grandpa was especially frustrated, he would say, "I wish Joe Brown woulda stayed off them railroad tracks and helped raise you niggas."

So I was a girl with all sorts of self-esteem issues going on. I wished I looked more like my sisters and my mother. I tried not to be klutzy. I wished family members didn't make me feel badly about being the daughter of a man who I had never met. The way they talked about him, maybe I was better off for not having known him.

I was never referred to by any terms of endearment—no sweetie pie, sugar, baby doll. No, the term that would linger in my mind for decades is *Joe Brown's seed*.

And I felt like something else was missing. My mother was a sweet lady; she didn't yell and curse at Vivian and me, but she followed the pattern of all the other adults by never showing us affection. All this made me feel like I was grasping for something that was just out of my reach— like I was trying to hold onto water with my hands.

I knew that my mother loved me, even if she never verbalized it. But in retrospect, I wished that I had had the love of a father, one who could have been a buffer between me and the cruelties of life—a guide through life from a man's perspective. I believe I would have been a better woman for it.

⸺ ❖❖❖ ⸺

Grandpa was a preacher, a cussing, itinerant preacher. On some Sundays, instead of going into town for church services, Grandpa would conduct service on the porch of our gray shack. The porch was wide enough to hold the whole lot of us, including Uncle Buddy and his family, and Uncle Henry who wouldn't be paying attention to anything, except for maybe some bug crawling on the floor.

Grandpa's friend, old Mr. Moe, would attend our house church. He'd listen to Grandpa for a few minutes, and then promptly fall asleep. Someone would have to nudge Mr. Moe to keep him from falling over in the rickety chair and to keep him from breaking his neck.

"Mama, why does Mr. Moe come to Grandpa's church?" I asked Mama one Sunday after he went home. "If he's tired, why don't he just stay home and stay in bed?"

"I don't know why people do what they do, child," was Mama's response.

The summer of Rosalie's stay, while the church services were going on, she would be looking as mad as all get-out. Her face said, *Can't Grandpa just hurry up and get this misery over with?*

We would sing a few hymns. Grandpa would read a few Bible verses and then preach to us about needing to get our lives right so we could go to heaven. One Sunday, Rosalie asked Grandpa if there was cussing in heaven. Grandpa's answer was to send her to our room. This happened right in the middle of service.

I didn't like church either. It was excruciatingly boring. But I *did* like Sundays. Saturday was reserved for doing our personal chores, including helping Mama with the laundry. Sundays were slow and easy, and Monday, with its endless work, seemed a distance away. Whatever meat we had for dinner would be put on a platter with sweet potatoes around it. Mama usually made a pie or cobbler for dessert from the canned fruit.

Sundays were for taking naps or getting our hair plaited or sitting on the porch and singing songs. We'd play ball with Uncle Buddy's two boys and Thomas and his little brothers. We played hopscotch and hide-and-seek. And wherever I went, my Raggedy Ann doll had to come along.

I liked Sunday afternoons, too, because Raggedy Ann; our dog, Gus; and I were free to roam the pinewoods. It was the only time I didn't have to share space with another person. I would sit down in the grass and braid the grass just like I would braid Raggedy Ann's red hair. Gus loved the freedom of running around the trees while I relaxed.

One afternoon, as I was walking, I found the stack of women's magazines. When I found those magazines, I might as well have won a grand prize. I was probably the happiest girl in the whole state of Georgia. I looked around, wondering who might have left the magazines there. But there was no one around, so I considered myself the lucky owner.

I lay right down there in the grass and looked at each page in every one of the magazines. The next thing I knew, it was almost dark. I heard Mama calling me, so I ran home with my arms full of my newly found treasures.

My mother was waiting for me as I appeared out of the woods behind the house.

"What's all that you got there, child?" my mother asked. She took some of the magazines that I was struggling not to drop.

"I found these magazines in the woods. Mama, the clothes these women are wearin' are beautiful! I'm gone make dresses like these when I grow up."

"Well, I don't know about that, but I don't want you out there in them woods by yo'self no more. You don't know who or what could be out there. So you stay outta the woods. You hear me?"

"Yes, Mama," I said. But I didn't care if I couldn't roam the woods anymore, because I had my precious magazines.

*** ✦✦✦ ***

There were times when it seemed like even though Mother lived with us, she would move away in her mind, as if she were living in her own world. I guess that was her way of coping with our hard life in the backwoods of Georgia.

Grandpa was hard on Mother. I imagined that she missed life with her parents. I had never met my parental grandparents, but they were people of some financial means. Mama talked fondly of her father. She said he was a mulatto, just as my father had been. He was a barber and a kind man. He wore starched shirts, owned property, and had left his only child some money when he died.

Grandpa had gotten ahold of Mother's money and spent all of it. When Mother asked Grandpa what had happened to the money, he said, "We done ate that money and shit it out."

"Mama, why doesn't Mother hardly ever talk?" I asked one evening. Mama, Vivian, and I were sitting on the porch, and she was plaiting Vivian's hair. Rosalie liked to take advantage of those times because she could have the bedroom to herself.

"I believe this here hard life don't agree with Mother," Mama answered.

"That's just what I was thinking," I said, happy that I was smart enough to come to the right conclusion. "But, Mama, this hard life doesn't agree with any of us too much, right?"

"You right, but some people just stronger than others."

On one of those occasions, when Mother was in a talkative mood, she had told me that she used to have a lot of fun dancing when she was a young girl. She said her friends would tell her that she was the best ballroom dancer in town.

I had closed my eyes tightly and tried to conjure up images of Mother as a young girl, twirling around in a beautiful dress. Dancing. Having fun. I tried to see her laughing and happy, with a boy telling her that he loved her. Then I opened my eyes and looked over at my grandmother. She was rocking in the chair beside me. I stared at her, watching her as she licked her gums. She tucked her lips under her gums and made the chewing action that I had become accustomed to seeing her do. And she had that faraway look in her eyes.

Rosalie had taught me the word *melancholy*. It was a fancy word for *sad*, and that's how I felt as I watched my grandmother visit a better time and place. At least I hoped that's where she was. In fact, melancholy was a good word for describing much of our daily existence in the backwoods of Georgia.

Why had Mother married Grandpa? Was I going to end up like her when I got old? The very thought frightened me. I hoped I wasn't going to be a broken woman like my grandmother.

"Mother had a better life before she moved here and married Pa," Mama said. Mama said that Mother's mother had once come for a visit. My great-grandmother said about Grandpa, "I can't be bothered with that man. I'll go to hell behind him because I'll kill him."

Maybe Grandpa wasn't a mean man, but he sure was a *hard* man. And no one could feel his pressure harder than his wife. Mama had told me wistfully, "Before the depression, we all had a better life. We used to have a fine piano, and we all played that piano. But Pa had to sell it so we could eat."

"You used to play the piano, Mama?"

"Yes, I did," she said with a laugh.

Sometimes Mother would come out of her shell, like when she proudly presented me a hand-sewn dress for my tenth birthday. She had made it from the sack that the flour we used for cooking came in. She told me, "I made it, I washed it, I starched it, and I ironed it."

Mother wrapped the dress in a brown paper bag and tied a red ribbon around the bag. That dress would be my prized possession until I couldn't fit it anymore. And even after I had outgrown it, I would keep it neatly folded in my dresser drawer.

I had long legs, and on my tenth birthday, I was as tall as my grandmother, who seemed to have stopped growing when *she* was ten years old. When we picked peaches on Mr. Clover's plantation for extra money, she would stuff peaches in her bosom and bring them home for canning. I supposed God would have to forgive Mother for stealing because he knew how hard she had it.

I remember when we first came back to Georgia. Mother did something that I thought was very strange. She walked alone to town, to get *all* her teeth pulled because they had decayed.

Vivian and I had met Mother in the road on her way back from the dentist. We ran to her. Her jaws were swollen like they were filled with a bunch of marbles, and I wondered how a person could stand to have *all* her teeth pulled, walk several miles back home, and not be crying out in pain. I later learned the word that best described my grandmother. She was a *stoic* woman.

"You okay, Mother?" I asked. "You okay, Mother?" Vivian asked.

Mother nodded yes. She took both of us by the hand, and we walked the rest of the way home in silence.

CHAPTER 3

MAMA WASHED THE laundry outdoors in the big black kettle that sat on top of a fire. She used a long stick to stir the clothes around in the water. The soap was made from lye and the drippings from the meats that she and Mother cooked.

Before Mama could do the wash, Vivian and I had to get the water from the well behind the shack. The water would have minnows in it, which we had to remove. We used the well water for everything from cooking to cleaning our bodies, and that water *wasn't* clean.

We needed baths more often than we took them, which we did in a large tin bucket behind the shack with little privacy. During the winter, we bathed in the kitchen.

My sister and I also had the job of hanging the clothes on the drooping lines.

Mama was working hard, trying to earn our keep. But as I said before, I believe that Grandpa was tired of *everything and everyone.* I'd heard him talking to Mother one night when we were all at rest and the crickets were chirping.

"Mamie Lee need a husband and a home for her and her children," he said.

"Who?"

"Who what?"

"Who da husband?" Mother asked.

"I got somebody in mind," Grandpa said.

We all went to service at the First Missionary Baptist Church in the Bottom. Grandpa liked holding service at our house, but Mama and Mother also liked going to the more lively Baptist church. Going to church in town gave us a chance to socialize and get away from the backwoods for a while.

After church, we had a dinner guest, John Feaster, better known as Mr. Rooster. We all knew Mr. Rooster from seeing him around town. He was friendly with Grandpa, but I never expected what happened shortly after his visit.

On a blazing hot Saturday afternoon in August, a few days before my birthday, Grandpa pronounced my mother and Mr. Rooster husband and wife. The ceremony took place in front of the house.

Under cover of the locust tree, I watched my mother and Mr. Rooster get into position for the ceremony. I didn't want to be too close to what I believed to be a disaster in the making. Mama was holding a bouquet of roses as she stood beside Mr. Rooster. Mama had told me to stop calling him Mr. Rooster, but I thought of him as a bird that needed to fly away, so she couldn't make me stop calling him that in my mind.

Mr. Rooster was an average-sized man. I don't know who he borrowed his suit from, but the jacket was hanging on him like it belonged to a giant. The hem of his pants kissed the red clay dirt, and his hair looked as though it had been slicked down with a full jar of Vaseline.

Mama was pretty in a pink dress, the only nice one she owned. She had gathered her hair into a bun at the nape of her neck and her face was made up with items that she had bought from the five-and-dime store in town. Vivian and I dressed in our best, and Mama had combed our hair into ponytails with ribbons. But no matter how fine the three of us may have looked, Mama didn't appear to be all that happy. I thought she should be bright and cheerful like the smiling young brides in my magazines.

Uncle Buddy's wife, Aunt Pearline, stood beside Mama as her attendant, and Uncle Buddy was Mr. Rooster's best man. As I stood watching my mother and Mr. Rooster, I recalled my conversation with Mama that we'd had while she combed my hair on the morning of the wedding.

"Mama, do you want to marry Mr. Rooster?" I asked. I was sitting in the chair as she stood behind me, trying to bring some order to my thick hair.

"It's what I'm doin'. It don't matter if I want to or not."

I was so confused and suddenly very sad. I knew that the whole idea was my grandfather's. Didn't my mother have any control over her own life?

"But couldn't you tell Grandpa you don't want to marry Mr. Rooster?" I asked.

"Listen, Lilly. This is grown folks' business. You mind yours. And his name is Mr. Feaster. Call him Mr. Feaster."

"Okay, Mama," I said, resigned to my mother's fate. I was not quite ten years old, but I was developing an uneasy feeling about life. Using a stinking, fly-infested outhouse was horrible. Working as a slave was horrible, and so were many other facts of life. But my overriding problem was something intangible.

As daily family life unfolded, I started worrying that I would never have a choice or a say-so in how the events of my life would play out. I thought about Mama's arranged marriage and about Rosalie coming to a place she considered a mere step above hell. Was life for me going to be simply a series of miserable events over which I had no control?

--- ◆◆◆ ---

We had some *strange* relatives who lived *way* back in the backwoods of Georgia. They only came out of the woods two or three times per year. They were *real* country. Their last name was Knuckles. I thought we were bad, with four of us sharing one little bedroom, but five of the Knuckles shared one *bed*!

Once the Knuckles had invited us to their house for dinner. The meal had consisted of only meat. They had set a table of pig feet, chitlins, cow brain, and I don't remember what else. What I *do* remember is Grandpa cussing and fussing on the way home about riding all the way out to the back of the backwoods to eat a bunch of meat, which he chose not to eat any of.

"If all I wanted to do was eat a whole pile a meats, I coulda done that at home," he complained as we headed back home.

Mama had invited the Knuckles to the wedding. One of the girls' names was Pig. Yes, her real name was Pig. And that's what she ate like.

She was eating hordes of the reception food until Rosalie bumped her with her hip. "Get away from this table," Rosalie said.

Oh no, I thought, *if Grandpa finds out about this, Rosalie's gonna be in trouble again.* Grandpa didn't take kindly to us treating guests poorly.

No rings were exchanged during the wedding ceremony, but Mama and Mr. Rooster did jump over a broom. Jumping the broom is what slaves used to do. It signified sweeping away the old to make way for a new life.

Mama seemed to have relaxed after she said, "I do." One of the guests was sitting on the step playing the fiddle, and Mama was enjoying herself. She was laughing and dancing with Mr. Rooster. She wasn't even angry when Aunt Bessie mocked her for having "an arranged marriage."

Looking back, I don't know why Grandpa thought Mr. Rooster could be of any help to anyone; his only earthly possessions were his clothes and his two roosters, a big one and a little one. The little rooster almost got killed by the big one in a fight.

As for Mr. Rooster's sleeping arrangements, until he and Mama could get their own place, he was going to make a pallet on the floor in Uncle Henry's cabin. I wasn't a fan of Mr. Rooster. Mama had bought Vivian and me a brand-new bicycle a few days before their marriage. She had saved for a long time to buy us that bike. While we were just learning to ride the bike, Mr. Rooster sold it.

About two weeks after the wedding, Mama chased Mr. Rooster off the property with Grandpa's shotgun. She pointed the shotgun to the sky, shot once, and ran after the man as he gripped a rooster in each hand. Mama was yelling, promising that if he ever came back around, she'd shoot him to pieces.

Mr. Rooster's crime was that Mama had caught him kissing Vivian on the mouth. I was happy to see him go, and that marked the end of Grandpa's matchmaking days.

But even before Mama's disaster of a marriage, a real romance was blooming—one that, for the life of me, I could not understand.

One evening, not too long after the fight between Thomas and Rosalie, Thomas was brave enough to come to our house for a visit. Vivian, Rosalie, and I were sitting on the porch, listening to the one station we could get on the radio. Thomas was almost like the brother I wished I had, and I didn't like how Rosalie had treated him.

Thomas's father had left for Chicago to find work when his son was thirteen years old. His father had promised that, once he found work and a place to live, he would send for his family. The father was never heard from again. It was as if he had disappeared from the face of the earth. During the first couple of years after he left, Thomas's mother, Miss Foster, had desperately tried to find her husband. She would ask anyone who was migrating to or visiting Chicago if they could please find out where her husband was and send word back to her.

She never heard any word, so she left her children with her mother and took the bus to Chicago to try to find her husband. She made arrangements to stay with her cousin, Linda, on the south side of Chicago.

For four days, day and night, she searched churches, clubs, stores, and alleys. She stood outside of plants, searching the faces of the black men who entered and exited the buildings. She went without food and sleep, walking until her feet had corns and blisters.

On the fourth night, when Miss Foster had returned to her cousin's kitchenette apartment, Linda told her that maybe her husband had never come to Chicago. Maybe she would never know what had happened to her husband. Dejected and defeated, Miss Foster fixed her mind on getting back home and raising her children without their father.

Miss Foster and the children moved in with her parents and three younger siblings, making their house a very crowded place to live in. Thomas worked hard on the farm and for other people, and like us, he rarely went to school. But Thomas was smart and had managed to learn to read and write. His family was planning to move to Milwaukee to live near Miss Foster's brother.

Thomas told me he was going to finish school, and he was going to be the man that he had missed in his life all those years after his father left. He and his little brothers were among the few friends that Vivian and I had because the farms were so spread out, and we didn't have any school friends.

"Hey, Lilly. Hey, Vivian. Hey Rosalie," Thomas said as he approached the porch.

"Hey," we girls responded.

"Rosalie, I came to apologize for makin' a bad impression on you."

We all stared at Thomas. His hands were stuffed in his pockets, and his right foot kicked at the dirt road. The front of our house had no grass, only the red clay dirt.

He was now talking to Rosalie. "Can you come over here for a minute?"

Rosalie's face was scrunched up in a frown. She looked at us, sucked her teeth, and rolled her eyes. She got up slowly and took the few steps to where Thomas stood.

Thomas was now talking low, but we strained to hear him as he asked Rosalie if she would like to go to the annual church picnic with him.

She looked back at us, as if she didn't know what to say. "Well, everybody's going anyway, aren't they?" she asked.

"Uh, sure. I guess so. They usually do. I just wanted to know if you would be my special company. We can sit together while we eat."

Rosalie said, "I'm supposed to apologize to you for attacking you. And why you want me to be your company?"

"You don't have to apologize. I figure you was probably just havin' a bad day. Maybe the heat was makin' you act crazy."

I thought the word *crazy* was going to cause her to act crazy all over again, but she just looked over her shoulder at us again, with a little smile on her face.

Turning back to Thomas, she told him she had to ask Grandpa if being his company was okay.

Rosalie surprised me. I had seen her as a tough-talking, tough-acting, smart city girl. Suddenly I was seeing her as well … a female.

We could see Grandpa through the screen door. He was sitting in the house in the old rocking chair, reading the Bible. A wad of chewing tobacco filled his jaw. I always wished someone could convince my grandfather to stop chewing tobacco. It was *so nasty*. He would have a tin can next to his foot, filled with spit. Often, one of us would accidentally kick the slimy, brown mess over, and *we* would have to clean it up!

Rosalie opened the screen door and entered the house to talk to Grandpa. When she reappeared, she told Thomas that, yes, she could be his special company at the picnic.

— ♦♦♦ —

In order to get to where the colored people lived in town, we had to travel to the edge of town to the Bottom. It was an area at the end of a hill.

The residents of the Bottom had a little more money and possessions than those of us who lived in the country. Actually, some of those people had a lot more money than we did. Some of the families in the Bottom owned property and a few businesses, like the funeral parlor. The Bottom was also home to schoolteachers with college degrees, a Negro doctor, and a couple of college professors.

Grandpa was nice to people who didn't live with him, and he was friends with a lot of the people in the Bottom. Being a preacher, once in a while, he performed a wedding or a funeral. When Miss Jenkin's baby died shortly after birth, she and Mr. Jenkins drove out to our house. Miss Jenkins, her face red from crying, held her lifeless child close to her heart. Mr. Jenkins asked Grandpa if he would "funeralize" the baby in two days. That would give anyone who was coming to the funeral time to do so. Miss Jenkin's face was so red and swollen from grief she was barely recognizable.

But my family was taking the ride to the Bottom on this Sunday morning for the happiest occasion of the year for the Negro residents of Malcom County, Georgia. Everyone would attend church, and dress in our Sunday finest. My finest was the flour sack dress that Mother had made me. I put ribbons on my plaits, and Mama had bought Vivian and me pink socks from the general store in town. It was too bad I couldn't get a new pair of shoes because the shoe boots I wore were too tight and squeezed my toes together.

Vivian wore a pink hand-me-down dress that had belonged to Honey. Rosalie and her mother had gone shopping before her trip to Georgia, so she wore a new red-and-white polka-dot dress.

After the service, the rows of picnic tables were covered with tablecloths and then the tastiest food that you could imagine. Mother had made her signature peach cobbler. Mama had made two wild berry pies. She would sometimes go out into the fields and pick the wild berries and her pies were delicious.

The picnic also featured a pig roast, potato salad, cold fried chicken, and watermelon, among other delicious treats.

And we played games. The small children ran around playing tag and hide-and-seek. The older kids hopped-raced inside giant potato sacks. We played stickball and danced to harmonica and banjo music.

Rosalie and Thomas only danced with each other. They didn't switch partners like everyone else did. They stuck close to each other the whole picnic, but they never went off alone like some of the other teenagers did. Grandpa would have taken a switch to Rosalie if she had done that.

It was close to dusk, and the festivities broke up. We got ourselves together and prepared to go home. In 1949 in rural Georgia, the KKK was a fact of life. We were well aware of crosses burning in front of black churches. We heard about lynching incidents. Looking back on it all now, I sometimes wonder how we were ever able to be happy. But I guess a person just has to cope with whatever the cards deal out. I suppose my perspective on life was shaped by things a bit differently from many other folks.

My family, Thomas's family, and Mr. Oliver's family were riding home in a caravan when we saw a raggedy colored man stumbling along the road, coming toward us. He had on one shoe, and when he saw us, he started running, waving his arms wildly.

The buggies and cars stopped. Miss Foster jumped down from their wagon and started running toward the man. A cloud of dust almost hid them from view as they fell to the ground in each other's arms. The raggedy man was Thomas's father.

Thomas came to visit us the next day.

"Where was your daddy for so long?" Rosalie asked him.

Thomas told us a terrible story about where his father had been and what happened to him. Mr. Foster and some other colored men were riding a train bound for Chicago. They hadn't gotten very far when, suddenly, a group of white men, with shotguns, boarded the train and forced all of them from the train. The men were taken to a plantation and made prisoners, or slaves as Mr. Foster saw it.

The men weren't paid for their work. They were in shackles every night and were fed just enough to keep up their strength to work. They were only occasionally allowed to bathe. This went on for several years, and then as suddenly as they were taken prisoner, they were set free.

"That's a scanous," Mama said. *Scanous* was another one of my mother's words, and I supposed that it meant *scandal*.

"I hate white people," Rosalie said.

My whole family was gathered on the porch.

"You got to love people," Mama said.

"They don't love us, Auntie Sweet. And how you gone love people who

treat us the way they do? We bleed red just like they do ... talkin' about
we ain't fully human. We have the exact same stuff on the inside of us as
they do." Rosalie was so bold. She talked to my mother in a way that it
never occurred to me to talk to her.

"The Bible say love yo' enemy and pray for those who spitefully
use you."

"I can't love those people. And I *won't* love those people. I'll *never* love
them."

Vivian was sitting on the step next to Thomas. He didn't seem like
he was paying any attention to what they were saying. He had a pained
expression on his face, as if he wanted to cry. Vivian put her small hand
on his shoulder.

"Don't be sad, Thomas. At least your daddy came home."

That day marked the first time I had seen a grown boy cry.

CHAPTER 4

❖❖❖

ROSALIE HAD PROBLEMS with pretty much everything about visiting us that summer; she was particularly angry about having to plow the field with the mule. And she pretty much had a problem with everything about Grandpa; she thought Grandpa was a ridiculous, backward old man. The fact that he made her do the plowing made her like him even less.

The ground had to be plowed to prepare for planting. Vivian and I could not plow with the mule yet because we were still too young, which I was very happy about.

And then the incident happened that scared all of us and gave Rosalie her reason to go home.

"This is the last time I'm comin' to this godforsaken place. If my parents try to make me come down here again, I'm gonna run away. The next time y'all see me, y'all gonna have to come visit me in Chicago," Rosalie had said.

Anyway, Grandpa had to go into town to the post office. Thomas wanted to go to the general store to buy some fabric for his mother for a birthday present. He wanted Rosalie to help him decide what pattern of fabric he should pick out. So Grandpa drove all of us kids in the wagon.

When we were at the counter to pay for the fabric, Mr. Bates accused Thomas of taking a dime off the counter.

"Mr. Bates, sir, I didn't take no dime. I got my own money. See."

Thomas tried to show him that he had the money to pay for the fabric, but Mr. Bates started yelling at him. Thomas started walking backward toward the door. The look on his face said that he couldn't believe what was happening. He ran out of the store, with all of us running after him, including Mr. Bates.

Everything happened so fast. Before we knew it, some white men had thrown Thomas in a car and were driving toward the Bottom. We all knew that there was a place near the Bottom where a colored man would be beaten and sometimes hanged.

Although I was only ten, I can still recall that day Thomas was almost lynched. Rosalie stood in the street, her hands covering her face, her voice full of hatred, outrage, and fear. "I can't believe this is happening!" she screamed. "Are you all crazy down here?"

I ran to her and held her in my skinny little arms. I felt her heart beating against my skin. I smelled her sweat. I smelled her pure rage and fear. "Come on, Rosalie," I said. "We got to get you off the street right now. It ain't safe."

Rosalie and I moved to the sidewalk, and I told Vivian to run to the post office to get Grandpa. He had already seen what was happening and had gone to get the sheriff. Grandpa instructed us to wait in the wagon.

We waited for what seemed like forever. At first, the three of us girls were all crying. But then our tears dried up, and we sat in silence.

I wondered what kind of shape Thomas would be in, if and when the sheriff and Grandpa brought him back. Would his body be pummeled and bloody? Would he be dead? I was scared. I didn't want to see a dead body, especially not Thomas's. And I was angry because people were going about their business as normal, as if our friend's life wasn't in danger, or it didn't matter.

He's gonna be okay, I told myself. *The sheriff is a nice man, as nice as a white man ever is to any colored people.*

Grandpa came back with Thomas in the sheriff's car. He was alive! His clothes were torn and dirty. He had some cuts and bruises, but he was alive.

Thomas's lips were moving, as if he were trying to talk, but couldn't get any words out. His whole body was shaking. The sheriff helped Grandpa get Thomas up into the wagon. He sat next to Rosalie. She stroked his arms and his hands. Her touch seemed to calm him and cause the shaking to decrease.

Thomas didn't deserve Mr. Bates trying to get him killed. He was such a nice boy. He never even got annoyed with his annoying little brothers.

"What did they do to you, Thomas?" Vivian asked.

"Hush, girl," Grandpa snapped.

We rode the rest of the way home in silence. Thomas's head was on Rosalie's shoulder. When we arrived at Thomas's house, Grandpa told his family what had happened. He said the sheriff told those men, "That boy wouldn't steal no money. They some good darkies."

"Lawd have mercy. Why is white folks so mean?" his grandmother asked.

Thomas's parents helped him down from the wagon, inspecting him. Even at my age, I hated the helpless, powerless feeling that we could have at the hands of white people.

The next day, Vivian, Rosalie, and I were sitting on the porch when Rosalie said, "I hate Georgia. Mama said she and Daddy are payin' for my bus ticket on Saturday, and I'm goin' back home Monday morning. I'm goin' back to Chicago, and I don't ever want to see Georgia again as long as I live."

Wiping tears away, she said, "I hate this place. Y'all don't have any running water, only that stupid water pump. And I hate that stinkin', nasty outhouse. Y'all don't have *anything* down here. And Thomas almost got killed." She shrieked the word *killed* and burst into tears.

Vivian and I looked pitifully at each other, about to cry ourselves. Mama and Mother came outside from the kitchen where they were canning peaches. Mother just stood on the porch with her hands on her hips, but Mama sat down beside Rosalie. She put her arm around her niece's heaving shoulders.

Poor Rosalie. She was a tough girl, but even a tough girl could only take so much. She had come to Georgia to get away from problems, only to encounter ones of a different kind.

Rosalie calmed down as Mama stroked her head. She looked Mama in the face. "Auntie Sweet, you know it's really awful down here. But you know something? It's hard in Chicago too. We live in a kitchenette apartment. The four of us live in two rooms and have to share a bathroom with everybody on the fourth floor of our building. Seems like everybody and their mama has moved to Chicago from the south. It's *so* overcrowded."

She perked up a bit. "But Mama said that we'll be moving soon. We'll have our own apartment." Gloom settled over her again, just as suddenly as it had lifted. "White folks don't like us in Chicago, just like they don't like us down here. I hate white people."

"Rosalie child, I do understand how you feel, but you cain't be hatin' on people. Jesus said you got to love yo' enemies. You got to learn to forgive people—even them men who tried to hurt Thomas."

"They were gonna *kill* him," she shouted.

"I know. But praise the Lord, it didn't happen. And you still got to forgive them."

"Did your mama and daddy straighten out their problems?" I butted in.

"I don't know. I don't care," Rosalie barked. "All I know is I'm goin' home."

"Won't you miss Thomas?" my little sister asked.

"Even if I will, I'm still goin' home."

••• ❖❖❖ •••

It had been three days since the *incident*. We hadn't seen Thomas or anyone in his family during that time. But now, here he was, walking up the road, his twin brothers in tow. The boys were miniature versions of Thomas.

The boys, Johnny and Jack, rarely wore shoes, and when they did, they might as well not have because the shoes were all busted up. One little boy was making a line in the dirt as he was dragging his baseball bat. The other boy was tossing a tattered baseball in the air.

We all greeted one another. After inquiring about Thomas's welfare, Mama and Mother went back to their work. Without a word, all of us kids started playing ball in the road.

After a few minutes, Thomas started talking. "My pop said I cain't go into town anymore, and I'm goin' to live with my people in Milwaukee in a few weeks. My uncle is gone send for me." He pitched the ball to one of the twins.

Thomas was always talking about moving to Milwaukee, but I started to wonder if that was really going to happen.

Rosalie stayed with us from the end of June to the beginning of September that year. Before she boarded the train for her trip back home, she and Thomas embraced and kissed right in front of us, including Grandpa. I was shocked. Vivian and I had sort of been Rosalie and

Thomas's chaperones all summer, and never had they even so much as held hands. I had no doubt, with that bold move, that they loved each other.

My cousin had made a great impression on me, and I did miss her after she went back home to Chicago. She had a fiery personality, and she was the first person I had met who had tangible goals for her future. I believed that if Rosalie could become something, I could as well.

CHAPTER 5

❖❖❖

WE HAD SURVIVED two more cold winters. The potbellied stove was fed with wood that the men chopped. We huddled around the stove until bedtime and then buried ourselves under Mama and Mother's quilts. Still, we suffered from the cold of winter, just as we did from the heat of summer.

In 1951, the Korean War was raging. Uncle Buddy's oldest son, Leo, was twenty-one, and he was drafted into the war. I was worried that he would be killed or come home the way Uncle Henry had; I almost didn't know which was a worst fate.

Uncle Henry lived in a tiny cabin behind our house. He would always be saying, "Hey, Joe. Hi, Joe. How you doin', Joe?" Maybe Joe had been a real person, someone who Uncle Henry had seen killed in combat. We didn't know because he didn't talk about his experiences. I remembered the pained look on his face when we'd greeted him upon his coming back from the war. There seemed to be no joy in being home. He retreated to his cabin and to his own little world. But he did work in the fields with us, planting and picking. While the rest of us sang as we worked, he mumbled to Joe.

When Mother or Mama fixed a meal, Vivian or I would run a plate out back to him and quickly run away from his cabin because we were afraid to be alone with my uncle.

On one afternoon when the air was still and full of its usual humidity in the midsummer heat of Georgia, instead of working in the fields, I was lying in bed and feeling ill. The sun shone into the room I shared with my sister and Mama.

My mind was doing flip-flops along with my stomach. I supposed I had eaten something that didn't agree with me. I was thinking about my life. I'd just turned twelve, and somehow my life didn't seem the same. It was like I was grown up already, and yet I still felt like a little kid. How was I ever going to make something of myself if I couldn't go to school on a regular basis?

Suddenly, I heard a gunshot. The bang echoed off the loblolly pines that surrounded the house. "Oh my God!" I whispered. "What now?"

I got up, pulled on some clothes, and ran out of the shack toward the origins of the shot. I assumed Uncle Henry was working. I kept walking, following where I thought the bang had come from.

When I found it, *it* was Uncle Henry. He was sprawled out in the field, his head lying in a puddle of blood, Grandpa's shotgun lying by his side.

The last thing I remember was screaming at the top of my lungs.

I had passed out, and when I woke up in my bed hours after discovering Uncle Henry's body, Mama was fanning me with a piece of paper and staring at me like I was some sort of alien. When I realized why Mama was sitting beside me, staring at me, I sat up in the bed and grabbed her tightly.

The horror of all the blood and Uncle Henry's eyes frozen wide open—I started shaking uncontrollably. My knees were knocking, which they always did whenever I was nervous, anxious, or afraid. Mama made me feel warm and safe as she hugged me, causing the shaking to subside. I was twelve, but she stroked my hair and rocked me like I was a little baby.

When the news of poor Uncle Henry's suicide spread to our family members who had moved away, they began converging on our little shack. There was no hotel for a black person to stay at in town, so some of the relatives stayed with Uncle Buddy, and others made pallets with the colorful quilts in our shack and slept on the floor. The rest stayed in my dead uncle's cabin. Mother sat on the porch humming and moaning. She rocked in the rocking chair while Grandpa and the other adults made funeral arrangements.

Uncle Henry's body was at Mr. Porter's funeral home in the Bottom. I had an uneasy feeling about Mr. Porter, maybe because of what he did for a living. He dressed in fancy suits and shiny shoes. He had a crooked grin and Mama said the devil was mixed up in that grin. The adults said he took advantage of his own people by overcharging for his services.

But he and Grandpa were friendly, so Mr. Porter offered him a discounted rate. Grandpa had done Mr. Porter the favor of preaching funerals a few times at his funeral parlor for people who had no church affiliation.

Grandpa owned two sets of clothing—a faded shirt and a pair of patched up overalls and the suit he wore for Uncle Henry's funeral. Uncle Henry also owned two sets of clothing. His patched-up overalls and a tattered shirt were his everyday attire. His other articles of clothing were the bloodied pajamas that he had died in. Grandpa had said, "Just bury him in pajamas."

Auntie Eula Mae was horrified by that idea. "That is no dignified way to bury family. We're just gonna clean his overalls and his shirt. That's what we'll bury him in."

On the day of the funeral, the sky was heavy with clouds, threatening a soaking rain. Our little house was crowded with people coming to bring food and express their condolences.

When Honey walked into the house, my eyes almost popped out of my head. Honey, whose real name was Vera, was twenty-one. She had moved to Atlanta as soon as she turned eighteen. Her words had been, "As soon as I turn eighteen, I'm outta this hick town. I'm movin' to Atlanta." Like Rosalie, she couldn't stand Grandpa or our country living.

Haynesville, with all its limitations, was too small and country for her. She had always been a wild child and unpredictable. But I hadn't expected *this*. It had been at least a year since I had seen Honey, and now, here she was with her stomach so full she was about to burst out of her floral-print dress. A strange little man with a receding hairline came in behind her.

Honey came around to each of us and introduced her husband, George Green.

I was flabbergasted. Honey hadn't been good about keeping in touch with us, but I thought she would have informed us about something as important as getting married and having a baby.

"Hi, Honey. I missed you," I said. Patting her stomach, I said, "I didn't know you was havin' a baby."

"I wanted to surprise you all, and I missed you too." Honey reached over to give me a hug.

"Hi, Honey," Vivian said, taking her turn patting the swollen belly.

Honey was beautiful, the prettiest girl I had ever seen. Her hair swayed across her back when she walked. Her silky, smooth skin was the color of dark honey, and she had large, brown eyes. She probably could have had her choice of a thousand men in Atlanta. Why had she chosen this little balding grinning man?

"Honey, when are you havin' your baby?" Vivian asked.

"Any day now," she answered, looking at her husband and smiling.

George Green smiled at us. I got the creeps.

I *was* happy to see my sister, but not this odd man. I had questions for Honey, and I couldn't wait to be alone with her so that I could ask them. Mainly I wanted to know why she hadn't told anyone she was married, with a baby on the way.

I didn't get a chance to ask my sister anything because she promptly went into labor. And to top it off, Mother told me to stay behind to help her and Auntie LaRue deliver Honey's baby. What a time for my grandmother to decide to come alive and talk!

I immediately thought of Rosalie and Rhonda, who had come to town with their parents for the funeral. Both girls were older than me. Why hadn't Mother told them to help?

Rosalie was happy to see Thomas, but she didn't act like she cared that Uncle Henry was dead.

Thomas's family was still working toward their big move to Milwaukee. Being sharecroppers made getting enough money together for a move difficult. Grandpa said that colored folks always owed the landlord money at the end of cotton-picking season. "You cain't ever get ahead," he would always lament.

Mama and Vivian were already crammed into the car with Uncle Buddy and his family. I ran out of the house to talk to Mama. My uncle's car was lined up behind Grandpa's wagon. He had transported Uncle Henry's body to the Bottom in his wagon. The wagon was my grandfather's only form of transportation.

It was drizzling now and not cold out, but I was shaking again.

"Mama, I wanted to go to the funeral with y'all, but Mother said I have to stay here and help deliver Honey's baby." My face was wet from rain and tears. I had already endured discovering my crazy uncle's dead body. Now I had to help deliver my sister's baby that she was having by a stranger. And what did I know about delivering babies anyway?

"Rosalie is older than me. Why can't she stay and help deliver the baby? Or Rhonda. I don't want to deliver no baby," I protested. "I'm scared." And at that moment, I was in a full-on crying fit.

But no one seemed to care.

"Do what Mother said, Lilly," Mama told me.

All eyes in Uncle Buddy's car were on me.

"But, Mama!"

"Go on, Lilly," Grandpa said, looking over his shoulder at me, holding the reins of his mule. I remember that his voice was tender as he told me to go on.

Defeated by the adults, I obeyed. I walked slowly back to the house as everyone started driving to the Bottom to bury Uncle Henry.

George Green was hanging around the front of the house, puffing on a cigarette as his wife was screaming through a contraction.

Honey was lying on Mother's bed, wearing the black dress she had changed into for the funeral. Her face was wet, and she couldn't keep still.

"Lilly, yo' job is to wipe Honey's face and hold her hand," Mother said. "She probably gone squeeze yo' hand real hard, and it's gone hurt, but this baby gone come soon."

Mother did more talking while Honey was having her baby than she probably had in ten years.

A clap of thunder caused me to jump. I thought about my family and Uncle Henry. It hadn't rained all week. Why now?

Honey's scream brought me back to her. After her contraction, she started crying. She put her arm under her back.

"My back. My back hurt so bad," she whimpered and moaned, arching her back.

"Honey, open your legs. I wanna see if I can see the baby's head," Auntie LaRue said.

"My back," she cried again.

"Honey!" Auntie LaRue said sharply. She pushed Honey's legs apart and looked.

"Listen, girl. I want you to scoot your behind to the edge of the bed. With your next contraction, I want you to push as hard as you can. I see your baby's head."

Auntie LaRue was so cool. It was as if she delivered babies every day.

Mother was standing at the foot of the bed, holding a quilt, ready to take the baby.

"My back hurt *so bad*."

I dipped the rag in the bowl of cool water; squeezed it out; and wiped her tears, her forehead, her cheeks, and her lips. I felt so bad for her and wanted to cry myself. I wondered how any woman could stand going through the pain of childbirth.

"Oooooohhh." Honey's scream ripped through the room and traveled out to her husband.

By the time she was finished screaming, her baby boy was out. After a whack on the behind, the baby was wailing.

Auntie LaRue turned around and tended to the baby, and then she held him up for us to see.

My mouth hung open because again I was shocked. The baby was white. I had seen newborns before, and if the parents were brown, the baby never came out white. I let go of Honey's hand because I was about to run outside to get George Green, but Auntie LaRue stopped me.

Auntie LaRue gently gave the child to his mother, and she sat down on the bed herself. We were all silent as she inspected her boy.

"Honey, does this baby belong to Mr. Green?" Auntie LaRue asked. She was always direct like that.

"No, the baby doesn't belong to Mr. Green. The man who is the baby's father got killed in a fight over a card game, so Mr. Green really liked me, and he asked me to marry him. He told me that he would be the baby's father."

I was standing by the door, confused. I truly did not understand the ways of adults.

"Well," Mother said, "you may as well go get the man."

I hurried out to get the stranger who had done a kindness for my sister and my new nephew. He threw his cigarette butt on the ground and followed me into the bedroom.

After George Green admired the baby and Honey said that the baby's name was George Jr., we cleaned up mother and baby. Honey changed into one of the nightgowns she had in her suitcase. I had been so upset about missing the funeral and terrified about seeing a baby born. When it was all over, though, I was happy to experience seeing a new life come into the world, and I felt a little more mature.

Mother and baby fell asleep, and we started getting ready for the repast. A pot of water was boiling on the potbellied stove for coffee. The angry rain had since stopped, so we arranged the food on a table out in front of the house just as had been done for Mama's marriage to Mr. Rooster. We covered the food with a tablecloth and sat on the porch waiting for everyone to return from the funeral.

They said Grandpa cussed the mule out the whole way to the funeral and the whole way back home.

The night of the funeral, the porch was filled with relatives talking about the day's events. Mama surprised me by asking Vivian and me if we wanted to leave with Auntie Eula Mae and her family when they headed back for Chicago in the morning.

"You mean go to Chicago to live?" I asked.

"No," Auntie Eula Mae chimed in. "To visit for a few weeks. You've been through a lot with Henry passing, and we think you girls could use a change of scenery. It will be good to get away for a while."

Of course we wanted to go and see the place that we had heard so much about from people who had migrated up north. I was nervous about going to Chicago because everything I'd heard wasn't good. But it was different, and the only place I had ever been was Buffalo. My aunt told us not to bring anything. I knew she meant that we didn't have anything worth taking with us.

⚛ ◆◆◆ ⚛

Our ride to Chicago alternated between joyful and vexing. Auntie had a book called *The Green Book*. Jim Crow laws were still in full effect, and many establishments refused to serve or accommodate Negroes. Although the Jim Crow laws were established in the South, the spirit of the law was pervasive throughout the country.

The book listed places where Negroes could eat, sleep, get gas, and use the bathroom instead of having to pee on the side of the road.

Uncle Willie Earl had relatives living in a town in Kentucky, and we stopped there to spend the night. The family consisted of a husband, wife, three young kids, and the wife's parents. They prepared a feast for us and more food for the remainder of our trip. What I remember most was how tender the father was with his little girl, and I wondered why Rosalie's father couldn't have been more like his cousin.

Auntie Eula Mae was normally unruffled, but she was very nervous about our road trip. She constantly encouraged her husband to drive faster. She didn't want to be caught in any town past sundown because she didn't want us winding up being sport for evil white supremacists.

"Hush, woman, and let me drive," Uncle Willie Earl would respond to his wife's nagging.

When we arrived in Chicago, I was struck with wonder. I was amazed that Chicago and the backwoods I had just left were in the same United States of America.

Rosalie laughed at Vivian and me, as our mouths were open, eyes wide, staring out the car windows at the Chicago skyline. "Y'all country bumpkins haven't ever seen anything like this before, have you?"

"Stop teasing, Rosalie," Auntie said. Then she pointed out some of the buildings to us. "That's the Temple Building. It's a church."

"Wow, that's a church?" Vivian said of the building whose steeple stretched toward the heavens.

As we passed the Wrigley Building, situated near the Chicago River, she told us that was the headquarters for the makers of the famous chewing gum. I was fascinated with the four clocks on the building and the many other skyscrapers in the city.

"Well, we're here girls," Auntie Eula Mae said as we entered the Negro neighborhood where her family lived. "Now, it's been a long ride. We're all gonna go into the apartment, take turns taking a bath, take a nap, and then we'll go out to eat."

Outside of their apartment, there was grass, and there were yellow and white flowers on both sides of the concrete steps. Inside was a small living room with walls decorated with flowered wallpaper. At home, our walls were covered with old newspapers.

Auntie Eula Mae continued the brief tour by showing us the brightly colored kitchen and the bathroom. During our stay, I would get in trouble with my aunt for lingering too long in the bathtub. When a girl goes from the outhouse to a place where she can lounge in a luxurious bubble bath, well, a little trouble is worth it!

Rosalie and Rhonda's bedrooms were small but neat. Auntie Eula Mae had her girls share Rhonda's room, and Vivian and I shared Rosalie's room.

Rosalie's twin bed was covered in a pink eyelet blanket. A multicolored quilt made by Mother lay folded neatly at the foot of the bed. There were two white dressers, and dresses, skirts, and blouses hung in the small closet. On the floor of the closet sat dress shoes, tennis shoes, and sandals. I didn't know how they had lived previously, but to me, they were now living in the lap of luxury.

Auntie Eula Mae gave Vivian and me each a suitcase full of clothes, which her daughters had outgrown. When alone, I closed the bedroom door and took all the clothes out of the suitcase. I sat them on the bed so that I could look at and touch each item. Getting the clothes reminded me of finding the magazines in the field.

Their apartment was such an amazing contrast to our dimly lit home in the backwoods. I immediately wanted to become a permanent resident of my relatives' household.

Auntie Eula Mae said we needed some exercise after having spent so much time in the car. After napping and refreshing ourselves, instead of driving to the restaurant, we headed out on foot in search of dinner. We passed by apartment buildings where girls were playing hopscotch and jumping rope on the sidewalk and boys were tossing balls to each other.

The south side of Chicago was street after street filled with stores, churches, and nightclubs and *so* many black people. How could one area hold so many people? I supposed that the area housed more Negroes than the whole state of Georgia.

My sister and I held hands as we walked behind Rosalie and her sister, who were walking behind their parents.

The streets got noisy as we left the residential area behind. Everyone seemed to be dressed up, and it was only Tuesday. No one wore overalls or potato sack dresses like we did back home.

My aunt worked as a secretary in an insurance agency. Uncle Willie Earl washed dishes at a diner, and he also worked at a meatpacking plant. Auntie Eula Mae and her husband didn't see too much of each other, and I guessed that was how they could get along. No one talked about him not believing that Rosalie belonged to him, but I could definitely feel a tension in the air.

Rosalie was seventeen and had a part-time job at Miss Brown's grocery store. Miss Brown was a colored lady who didn't look like she was much older than my cousin. Whenever I went to Miss Brown's store, I couldn't help but stare at her as she worked. She would inspect the apples in the barrel or ring up a customer's order with her big black cash register. A young Negro woman owned a grocery store! I was fascinated.

We were eating dinner our second evening in Chicago. "I've made arrangements for our next-door neighbor to keep an eye on you girls while everyone's at work," Auntie Eula Mae said.

"Why do we need a babysitter?" I asked. "I'm twelve, and Vivian is ten."

"I'm well aware of how old you girls are. But you *are* in a strange city, and I just would prefer that you have someone to keep an eye on you. Miss Cat can use some company herself. We'll go over so you can meet her after dinner."

⸺ ◆◆◆ ⸺

The next afternoon, we went over to Miss Cat's apartment. She was an old lady who wore flowery housedresses, and she laughed a lot, even about things that didn't seem comical to me.

"She's strange," Vivian whispered in my ear as we helped her make sandwiches and lemonade. "Why is she always laughing?"

"I don't know," I said, hunching my shoulders.

Miss Cat had a lot of pictures sitting on the end tables and hanging on the walls in her apartment, so I thought it was strange that she never had any visitors, at least not while we were with her. Her companions were her cats, Bobby and Billy.

Her only child, Mason, and his wife and two baby girls, had been killed in a car accident while driving to Chicago from Memphis, Tennessee. Her husband had died from cancer shortly after the son's death.

Like Vivian said, she *was* a bit strange. But I liked Miss Cat and hoped that she had other companions besides her cats. We were feeling more comfortable with Miss Cat and started asking her questions. I asked her if she had any friends.

"I do," she said cheerfully. "I visit them sometimes and they visit me sometimes, and I see them at church on Sundays. And your auntie is really sweet to me. And Jesus. There's no closer friend than Jesus."

Her response made me feel better.

"How come they call you Miss Cat?" Vivian asked. We ate chicken sandwiches and drank too-sweet lemonade. "Is it because you love cats?" Vivian continued.

Miss Cat let out a hearty laugh, showing us her tiny yellow teeth. "No, baby. My real name is Catherine, spelled C A T H E R I N E. So Cat is short for Catherine. My brother started calling me that when I was a little bitty girl. The name just stuck to me."

"Where's your brother now, Miss Cat?" I asked. I rubbed Billy's head. He was the fat brown and white cat. He went crazy at the smell of chicken, so Miss Cat would always shred some and put it into his dish. She was always fussing at those cats, but she loved them.

"I lost my brother in a house fire a couple of years ago. He was all the family I had left."

"Oh," we both said. I didn't know how she could be so cheerful after so much loss.

Fear is such a sneaky emotion. I hardly noticed it creeping up on me and taking up residence in the corners of my mind. Miss Cat telling us about the tragedies in her family solidified my belief that there was precious little in life that a person could control.

I was already aware that a poor Negro person had little say so in where they lived or what they did for a living. Even in Chicago, we had precious few choices in what parts of town we could live. Now I realized that I could die from a car accident on the way back home to Georgia. Or I could get sick and die.

The one thing that I felt I had total control over was my dream of becoming a fashion designer, and I spent hours devouring my aunt's magazines. She kept a stack of *Ebony* magazines and the *Chicago Defender* newspaper on the living room coffee table and made them required reading. The women's hair in the magazines was perfectly coiffed, their makeup was expertly applied, and they were fashionably dressed.

Some of the women wore very revealing swimsuits. But I could relate to all of them because they were women with my complexion and with my sisters' and mother's complexion. Seeing how the women in Chicago and the women in the magazines dressed made me know that there was a demand for women of color to be dressed well, and I was going to help them to do that.

For the remainder of our trip, I was able to keep my fears at bay. There was a lot to distract me, lots of amazing firsts for my sister and me on our weeks-long visit to Chicago. One of the more memorable firsts for me was when Auntie Eula Mae straightened my hair. Hardly any of the girls in Chicago wore plaits in their hair, which was our main hairstyle back home.

The Saturday afternoon after our arrival in Chicago, after lunch and chores, my aunt decided that, since we were in the big city, we needed a big city hairdo.

"Go sit down in the kitchen," she told me after she had washed my hair and it had been dried with her noisy hair dryer. I watched her put a funny-looking comb on the stove and turn the fire on.

"What's that?" I asked.

"It's a hot comb. I'm gonna straighten your hair out. Rosalie will be home from work soon, so she'll roll it up for you. You'll have some pretty curls for church in the morning."

Auntie Eula Mae combed my hair, parting it into sections and greasing my scalp and hair with Royal Crown. She then slathered my hairline and my outer ears with Vaseline. Next she started pressing my hair.

But she was *frying* my hair! It was crackling and smoking as the comb made its way down to the ends of my hair. The comb touched my ear. I jerked. "Ouch!"

Vivian was standing by the icebox, watching with her mouth open.

"I'm sorry, Lilly," Auntie Eula Mae said. "Hold your ear down, and hold still. It's just a tiny burn. You'll be okay."

I held my ear. My head was tilted to the side, my shoulders were tight, and I was ready to jump out the chair if that hot comb singed my ear again. Fried hair has an odd, stuffy burning odor.

"So what do you girls think about Chicago?" my aunt asked.

"It's big," I said.

"And so many people," Vivian chimed in.

I was enthralled with Auntie Eula Mae. Our small town definitely could not contain all of what she was. She was a fancy lady. I wouldn't have called her beautiful, but she painted her lips and nails red, and she was a self-assured woman who carried herself like a queen. If I wanted to be like anyone when I grew up, it was my aunt.

"God didn't make us to be slaves," she said as she straightened my hair. "A person can't be who they were meant to be slavin' on a farm down south."

"Auntie, do you hate white people?" I asked.

"Why do you ask me such a question, Lilly?" said Auntie Eula Mae.

"I was just wondering. Rosalie said she hates white people, but Mama told her she has to love everybody."

"Yeah," Vivian said. "When Thomas told us about the bad things that happened to his daddy, Rosalie said she hates white people. And she said it again when Thomas almost got killed by those white men."

"I know about those terrible, awful things that happened. People do hateful things, white people and Negroes. But I just choose to believe that there are *way* more good people in the world than there are bad, on both sides. And Sweet is right, we have to ask the Lord to help us to love our neighbors, no matter who they are."

Auntie Eula Mae turned the stove off and said, "But your question was, do I hate white people, and my answer is *no*. But just like everybody, there are some that I don't like."

After my aunt finished frying my hair, she told me to go take a look in the bathroom mirror. Vivian followed me to the bathroom.

"It's straight like mine now," Vivian said as we stared at my thick red hair that now hung past my shoulders. I didn't know it was that long.

After we finished admiring my hair, it was Vivian's turn. She sat down in the kitchen while Auntie greased her scalp and brushed her hair one hundred times.

"Auntie, why do children who have the same parents come out so different from each other?" I asked.

"Have you asked your mother this question?"

"Yes, but she only said that it's how God made us. But I still don't understand. For example, why does my sister have good hair and I have thick red hair that needs to be straightened out?"

"Have you ever heard of genes?"

"You mean dungarees?"

"No, silly," my aunt said, laughing. "I'm talking about the genes in your blood. Everyone has genes in their blood that determine everything from the shape of your nose to the color of your hair."

"So I'm dark like Rosalie, and Lilly's light like Rhonda because of genes?" Viv asked.

"Yes. We inherit traits from our parents, and sometimes what one parent passes on to us is stronger than what we get from the other parent. You'll learn more about this as you go on in school. *And* there's no such thing as *good hair* and *bad hair*. Hair is hair."

"Wow. Look at you," Rosalie said when she came home from work. "So you finally got rid of those tired plaits."

"Rosalie, one of these days you're gonna say something nice to somebody. Lilly needs you to roll her hair up for her," Auntie Eula Mae said.

My cousin made curlers from a brown paper grocery bag. She cut the bag up into strips and rolled up my hair. Then she did the same for Vivian.

I couldn't wait for Sunday morning to see my hair, so when I was supposed to be asleep that night, I went to the bathroom and undid a few of the paper curlers. I gasped in amazement. I had Shirley Temple curls!

"Lilly, are you okay?"

I didn't know Auntie Eula Mae knew that I wasn't in bed. She had startled me back from my fantasy about having my picture taken and being in a magazine like the ones I had found in the woods.

"You've been in that bathroom an awfully long time."

"I'm coming out." I quickly rolled my hair back up, flushed the toilet, and scurried back to bed. But I was so excited I could hardly sleep.

Vivian and I were up at six o'clock in the morning. We fussed with our hair so much until most of the curls were gone. We rolled our hair back up and went to bed until it was time to get up for church.

Everyone went to church except Uncle Willie Earl. He went to his job at the diner. Miss Cat walked with us to Mt. Aaron Baptist church, a large redbrick building. It was like a parade to church as the sidewalks filled with people going to large edifices and storefronts alike, all dressed in their Sunday finest.

The service was stimulating, a great contrast from what we endured at home. The church was packed, including the balcony. The choir, swaying in their robes, clapped and sang stirring songs about going home to live with Jesus.

After church, Vivian and I went to the movies for the first time. Rhonda and Rosalie took Vivian and me to the movies to see a Jimmy Stewart movie. I tried to count how many boys and girls were waiting in line outside of the Regal Theater, but it was impossible, save to say that a lot of people went to the movies that day.

After the movies, we went home to Auntie Eula Mae's fried chicken dinner. Uncle Willie Earl came home to eat, and Miss Cat, who made a pound cake, ate with us as well. Uncle Willie Earl had a cigarette with his dessert. He tapped ashes into the glass cigarette tray that sat next to his coffee cup, and he blew smoke right into my face.

At that moment, I started a mental yes and no list for when I grew up and married. I would have to fill in the yes side later, but my immediate nos were no chewing tobacco, no snuff, and no cigarettes. I would not consider marrying a man who engaged in those vices.

My aunt never said anything to her husband about his smoking habit. Instead she would keep the windows open and spray au de toilette around the apartment.

As the days passed, I found myself changed somehow. The city had a pull on me, as if I'd never been alive until that visit. I didn't want to return to Georgia and my life as a sharecropper, to picking cotton, to the outhouse, to all its insanity under Jim Crow and the KKK. At one point, Rosalie took Vivian and me to the community recreation center. Basketball and ping-pong were being played. A woman was teaching girls to crochet; she displayed some items that she'd made, including colorful afghans. I decided to learn to crochet and took yarn and hooks home to practice. I enjoyed crocheting and became good at it in no time.

Chicago summers were almost as hot as Georgia's.

"It's so hot outside you can fry an egg on the sidewalk," Rosalie said one Saturday afternoon when she came home from work.

"You fry eggs on the ground?" Vivian asked.

"No, silly. It's just an expression," Rosalie said. "Let's pack a lunch and go swimming."

We bought bathing suits at a huge Goodwill near their apartment and caught the bus to the Negro beach. Rhonda, who hadn't spent much time with us, came along. She was nineteen, worked at the post office, and said that she was going to marry her boyfriend, Alfred, once he graduated from college.

In 1910, there was a race riot on the beach in Chicago. The riot occurred because a black teenager had swum into the white part of the beach.

I couldn't swim very well, but I enjoyed floating. I would float on my back, look up at the sky, and think about God. Mainly I thought about God because people confused me. Sometimes I wanted to go to heaven so I could ask God questions. I wanted to know why people couldn't get along with each other. Why did they hate one another because of the difference in skin color? It made no sense to me.

I realized that there was much in life that was beyond my control, including death, poverty, and hatred. But no one could keep me from dreaming. I started taking my aunt's *Ebony* magazines with me to Miss Cat's apartment. Since I'd discovered that I was a decent artist, I would draw pictures of the women in the magazines and draw outfits resembling those in the magazines. I was going to become a dress designer. I had seen enough to know that not all African Americans were poor and uneducated. So I believed in my heart that it was entirely possible for my dream to come true.

CHAPTER 6

⬥⬥⬥

THE SUMMER IN Chicago marked a milestone for me. My time in the city opened my eyes to the wider world, a world where I believed I could make something of myself. I thought long and hard about that on the bus ride back to Georgia, and I dreaded the return to sharecropping, the backwoods, and the drudgery of a life that held no promise for my future. As the bus pulled into the station, I looked out the window and saw Grandpa standing there, his arms folded across his chest, a sour look on his face, as if he dreaded my return as much as I did.

But we returned home to find that we were no longer going to be slaving on the farm. My grandparents' children had put their money together and were having a house built in the Bottom for Grandpa and Mother. The siblings said their parents were getting too old to continue working in the fields. Vivian and I hadn't been told about it because they'd wanted to surprise us, and it was a wonderful surprise.

By the time we got home, the house was almost finished. The wooden house was painted white, quite a contrast from the drab little house in the backwoods. It had two bedrooms, a living room, a yellow painted kitchen, *and* a bathroom.

The house was situated on a large plot of land. Vivian and I bought a ball from the general store and while the house was being completed, we would run around playing kickball with some neighborhood kids until we were exhausted.

Finally, the day came for us to bid farewell to the backwoods for good. Moving day should have been a happy one. Instead, a cloud of gloom had been cast over the day. Mama told us that she was moving to Buffalo to live with her sisters. She was going to leave Vivian and me with our grandparents so she could get a job and find a place to live. Then she would come back to get us.

Panic washed over me. "Mama," I said, "that's what Thomas's father said. How you know the same thing won't happen to you that happened to him?"

She didn't respond to my question.

"Mama, can we *please* go with you?" Vivian pleaded. She grabbed Mama around the waist.

Mama pried Vivian's hands away. "Stop that, Vivian. Y'all girls are going to stay here with Grandpa and Mother. You gonna go to school, and as soon as I can, I'm going to come back here and get y'all."

We both started crying. Whenever I tried not to cry out loud, my throat would start hurting. But why shouldn't I cry? My mother was going away, and I didn't know when I would see her again. I felt like an orphan. My grandparents loved us, but they were old. And Grandpa definitely didn't want to raise any more kids.

I wanted to cling to Mama, like Vivian tried to do. But one thing I knew for sure about Mama was that, when she made up her mind about something, you might as well forget about trying to change it.

With our mother's impending move to Buffalo, my grandparent's new house had lost its appeal for me.

On moving day, as we took the quiet ride to town, with Grandpa driving Uncle Buddy's truck, my mind went back to when I was six years old. Mama had sent me away to live with her cousin, Vernon, and his wife, Hazel, so that I could go to school.

Cousin Hazel was a teacher who taught in a little school near their house. Living with Mama's cousins didn't last very long because I missed my mother terribly.

Cousin Vernon was a kind man. One day I was crying, and he had squatted down to get eye level with me. He asked me what was wrong.

"I wanna go home. I want my mama." I was miserable and wouldn't stop crying, so the cousins took me home to my mother.

But I wasn't six anymore. I knew that crying wasn't going to help anything. So I decided that I wasn't going to cry anymore about Mama going to Buffalo. I knew that she loved us and that she was doing what she had to do. I had to believe that we would soon be with her again. That is what I told Vivian.

We began to regularly attend the colored school in the Bottom. We still had to pick cotton when we needed money for things like school supplies and new shoes.

We also began going to the movies. Of course, we had to go around to the side of the building and sit in the balcony with the rest of the colored people. It cost a quarter to get into the theater, which showed a lot of cowboy movies.

We took our cowboy movies very seriously. A highlight was when, one Saturday, the actors came to town to perform live at the theater. One of the cowboys was missing from the act. A boy in the balcony shouted down, asking the others where the missing cowboy was. The response was that he couldn't make it. That the actors were there in person and talking to us was exciting.

I felt more dignified living in town. I started babysitting, which meant I had a little money to shop with in the ten-cent store. My favorite treat was orange soda water.

We were no longer experiencing the degrading poverty of our country life, and although Mother still wasn't the most talkative person, she did become more animated. The land the house was built on had pecan trees, and Mother planted more rows of trees, making the property a pecan farm. People admired Mother for planting all those trees. Someone called her an *entrepreneur*. I looked that word up in the dictionary and realized that Miss Brown in Chicago was also an entrepreneur.

Harvesting the pecans was a lot of work. We couldn't do it all ourselves, so Mother would hire a few men to assist us. We picked up the pecans from the ground as they fell from the trees and put them in pails. Once the pecans were cured and shelled, we sold them to stores in the county and to the townspeople.

One of the best things about moving to town was that Mother had bought a straightening comb, so we no longer had to wear our hair in plaits. We even went to the beauty parlor once in a while.

*** ❖❖❖ ***

The following year, Mama kept her word and came back for my sister and me. She stayed for a short while to visit with my grandparents, and then we were off to Buffalo. I never imagined that I would be sad to leave the Bottom, but I was. It was hard leaving my grandparents and my friends.

Thomas and his family had finally moved to Milwaukee. He gave me his address, and we promised to keep in touch. I was growing up and realized that everything was changing.

We said goodbye to Grandpa and Mother several days before Thanksgiving. I didn't like the idea of leaving them, but they still had Uncle Buddy. He was a big, tough man who would look out for them. Uncle Buddy's son had made it safely home after the war, and he too, had moved away. My grandparents, Uncle Buddy, and his family saw us off at the tiny bus station.

"Mama, are we ever gonna see Grandpa and Mother again?" Vivian asked, once we were situated in the back of the bus.

"Of course we'll see them again. Why you ask somethin' like that?"

"Because they're old, and we're movin' so far away. I just wanna be sure we'll see them again." Vivian was speaking so softly, it was like she was talking to herself. She turned to stare out the window. I was sitting with Mama, and Vivian was in the window seat ahead of mine.

Mama promised us that we would have a wonderful Thanksgiving meal with all our relatives who had moved to Buffalo. I had spent so much of my young life aching to move away from Georgia. Now that it was happening, I had mixed emotions. Since we were no longer living in the backwoods and breaking our backs picking cotton, moving up north didn't seem as important. But we were on the bus, passing towns and cities, and there was no turning back.

"Mama, do we have a house to live in?" I asked.

"We gone live in Bessie and Slim's house. They bought a house, and we gone stay upstairs with LaRue. Bessie and Slim live downstairs."

"But Mama, Aunt Bessie doesn't even like us. Why are we gonna live with them?" I protested.

"Hush, child. Don't be makin' no show on this bus."

My eyes welled with tears, and I pouted.

After a moment, Mama's voice softened. "We have to live there until

I can afford to get a place of our own," she said. "Like I said, we gone stay with LaRue. She has the upstairs apartment."

Living with Aunt Bessie! Misery washed over my soul. I felt worse than when Mama had moved to Buffalo without Vivian and me. At that moment, I wished that I were old enough to make my own decisions. It wasn't that I didn't love my mother, but things felt as if they were changing too much for me. As usual, I had no control over my circumstances.

"You like Buffalo, Mama?" Vivian asked as we ate cold fried chicken, bread, and goodies from the general store.

"I like it fine," Mama said.

For some reason, I didn't believe her.

I spent the majority of that long ride to Buffalo deep in thought about the major events that had shaped my thirteen-plus years of life. The low point, besides any day spent out in the unrelenting sun picking cotton, was when I had found my poor uncle Henry's dead body.

Reminiscing about my trip to Chicago lifted my spirits. Discovering that I had talent and enjoyment for working with my hands had buoyed my hopes that maybe good things could happen for me in Buffalo.

Auntie Eula Mae was the first person to tell me that I was talented. When she had seen me drawing while sitting on the floor in her living room, she asked to see what I was doing. It was one of my typical drawings. Initially, I traced pictures of women in the magazines, and then I moved to freestyle drawing, which bolstered my confidence in my creative abilities.

"This is pretty good, Lilly. You know, you're very talented. You're good with your hands. You see how quickly you picked up the crocheting, and you can make things without a pattern. You keep that up. Hobbies are good to have. Who knows? Maybe some of this will turn in to more than a hobby for you some day."

I was beaming. My aunt had been the first person to encourage me that way, and it was the initial push that I needed to propel my dreams forward. I knew I wasn't very book smart, but I was beginning to realize what my aunt meant. Working with my hands was enjoyable and felt natural.

Since I knew that it was cold in Buffalo, I figured out how to make a hat and scarf set. By the time we arrived in Buffalo, I had made an orange set for myself and a red set for Vivian.

Finally, after our long ride, where it seemed we stopped in half the towns in America, the bus pulled up to the station in downtown Buffalo. We stepped off the bus and out into the cold. *Everything* looked gray. Immediately, I wanted to go back down to the warmth and familiarity of Mother's pecan farm.

I was beginning to scare myself, wondering if I would ever be satisfied.

"We have to walk down here to the cabstand to catch a taxi," Mama said as we started down the street, carrying our heavy suitcases.

As I said, *everything* looked gray. The ground was gray. The buildings were gray. And of course, the sky was singing a mournful, gray song.

There weren't as many buildings, and those there were weren't as tall as in Chicago, but there were still lots of people walking around downtown, Negro and white. They were bundled up against the cold, carrying shopping bags.

Mama was carrying a heavy suitcase. Vivian and I were each carrying a beat-up suitcase, and Mama was holding Vivian's free hand like she was still a little girl. Mama was walking so fast we were practically running to keep up with her.

I was looking up at the names of the stores on Main Street. I saw a Woolworth's. There *was* a ray of sunshine in Buffalo after all!

"Look, Viv, they have a Woolworth's," I said.

"Oh yeah," she said.

"Mama. Mama, can we go in Woolworth's?" I asked.

The massive Woolworth's and the Goodwill had been my two favorite stores to shop at while in Chicago. Auntie Eula Mae bought most of her knickknacks from Woolworth's.

"We can go Friday after I get off work. Not tomorrow because it's Thanksgiving. So we can go Friday," Mama said.

Mama seemed agitated, and I started worrying.

"Are you okay, Mama?" I asked, as we reached the cabstand.

"I'm fine. It's cold out here, and I'm tired. The bus ride was too long, and I just want to get home."

Yes. I remembered. Mama sometimes would become cranky when she was overly tired.

We settled into the back of the taxi, and Mama told the driver where to take us. "One fifty-two Madison." That was our new home.

"Mama, does it ever get sunny in Buffalo?" I asked.

"Yes," she answered, almost smiling. "Yes, it gets sunny in Buffalo." Although my mother mustered up a slight smile, her behavior made me anxious. It was the same feeling I'd had while watching her marry Mr. Rooster. The anxiety began to crowd out any hopes for a happy Thanksgiving in my new hometown.

But we did have a nice welcome to Buffalo. Everyone gathered at Cousin Georgia's house. She and her husband had five kids. They owned a large home in the Cold Springs area. Their house was overrun with family and friends on that day, and my sister and I made fast friends with our cousins.

The dread that I had been feeling about coming to Buffalo almost seemed to be unfounded, as Aunt Bessie had mellowed out. She behaved as if she didn't mind having Vivian and me around.

But Aunt Bessie was still a party woman, and her house was party central. The weekdays were usually pretty quiet, reserved for the ladies whose hair she did for extra cash. She also had the numbers runners come during the day. I was infatuated with one of the handsome, young numbers runners. Auntie LaRue didn't play the numbers, but she said that Aunt Bessie and Uncle Slim bet on the horses.

The weekend parties were long, drawn-out affairs, filled with finger popping music, smoking, liquor, and card playing.

After Thanksgiving, Mama enrolled us in school. Vivian was still in grammar school, so she went to school number seven. I was a freshman, so I went to Fosdick Masten High School.

When I came home from school after the first day, I was excited. I had good news. Aunt Bessie didn't have any clients that afternoon, and she and Mama were sitting in the parlor watching a soap opera.

"Mama, guess what," I said.

"What, child?"

"I'm gonna take home economics. They're gonna teach us to cook and how to handle money and a lot of other things. But the best thing is I'm going to learn how to sew. I can make clothes." I had my schedule of classes, waving it in the air. I wanted to give it to Mama to take a look at, but unfortunately, she could barely read or write. She could read a few Bible scriptures and scratch a poor signature for her name.

"You remember that's what I told you I always wanted to do?"

Mama looked at me with no enthusiasm and little interest.

I continued anyway. "I can take sewing classes every day. They have classes where you can become a practical nurse too, but I want to design my own clothes. I can make them and sell them."

"Good," Mama said, focusing on the man and woman on the screen who were fussing at each other.

I started to ask Mama what was the matter, but she obviously didn't want to talk. So I just walked through the parlor and living room into the dining room. Vivian was sitting at the table. We said hi and did our homework in silence.

When Aunt Bess' husband, Uncle Slim, came home from work, he'd liven things up. He always entered the house through the kitchen door. His routine was to sit his empty lunch pail on the counter, wash his hands, grab a beer from the refrigerator, pop open the can, and take a long drink. Then he was ready to greet the household.

"Hey, girls," he'd say with a laugh. He would always kiss us on the cheek, his facial stubble scratching our skin. And he always smelled like violet breath mints.

Uncle Slim had to help support Vivian and me because, soon after we moved to Buffalo, Mama had another nervous breakdown. Somehow, I wasn't surprised. She always seemed agitated and not at all happy. She had started talking about bugs crawling up her nose and in her hair.

Mama wound up in a psychiatric ward in a building that reminded me of a scary old castle that you would see in the movies.

I was fourteen, the age you had to be to visit a patient. I thought Vivian was lucky because she wasn't old enough to be subjected to seeing our mother in her awful condition.

"You sure you want to see your mama?" Auntie LaRue asked me. "You know she's not herself. She might not even recognize you."

"Yes. I'm sure," I said. The honest answer was that I *didn't* want to see her in that condition, but I *needed* to see her. I missed Mama, and I missed my grandparents a great deal. With each passing day, I wasn't so sure about living in Buffalo.

With Mama gone, I almost felt as if I didn't have a home. And I hated just about everything about the city, especially the houses. I thought they were all ugly.

The worst house of them all was Aunt Bessie's. The wood was dark, and the house never seemed to have enough light. I could have sworn I saw a ghost floating around and imagined the ghost was the cause of the creaking noises in the house.

I was downright afraid every time I went in the bathroom. Unlike at Auntie Eula Mae's apartment, I did my business quickly and hurried out. The bathroom was long and narrow, with a floor that sloped. My wild imagination thought that someone had died in the bathroom, but I was told the floor sloped because the house had no basement.

The only thing that I *did* like about living in Buffalo was my sewing class. I was learning to read patterns, and my first project was to make a simple skirt.

Auntie LaRue, who never had any children of her own, took good care of Vivian and me when we stayed with her. She taught us to play a few songs on the piano, and she took us shopping and to church.

Auntie had moved to Buffalo when Vivian and I were little girls. She had been pen pals with a man from Buffalo. After she had corresponded with him for a while, he'd paid for a bus ticket for her. They'd married soon after her arrival, but the marriage had failed in short order.

Soon after they'd separated, Mama, my two sisters, and I traveled to Buffalo to live with Auntie LaRue. We all crowded into a dreary little two-bedroom upstairs apartment, which had no closets. The kitchen had one light bulb; a small table with two chairs; and a faded, curled-up-at-the-edges linoleum floor. As a bonus, bedbugs accompanied us to bed every night. That was my first experience with Buffalo.

Auntie LaRue and I visited Mama on an unusually hot, late March day, after school. The mental hospital had a courtyard with some picnic tables, and we sat at one of them while waiting for Mama. The nurse had told us that Mama needed some fresh air, so they were bringing her out to us.

A man and woman, who were dressed in white, brought her out to the courtyard, and she sat down on the bench across from us. The attendants stepped back with their hands folded.

I sat on the bench next to my aunt. When I saw my mother, she may as well have been a stranger. Her hair was matted down in the back and on the sides and sticking up on the top of her head. Her eyes were wide and rolling back and forth, and I knew she didn't know who her own child was.

"Hi, Mamie Lee. How you doin'?" my aunt asked.

Of course there was no answer. But I took the queue from my aunt. "Hi, Mama. How you doin'? It sure is nice outside for October. I hope you can get better so you can come home soon. We miss you ..." My voice trailed off. I thought I sounded ridiculous talking to a woman who didn't even seem to know I was there, much less who I was.

Couldn't somebody at least comb her hair? I thought. My mind went back to the Sundays on the creaky, wooden porch in Haynesville. Mama would part my hair and plaster my scalp with Vaseline. She would brush it into submission one hundred times, and then she would make four plaits.

"Auntie, can't somebody do Mama's hair?" I asked in a low voice.

"I will come back here tomorrow after I leave work. I'll do her hair."

"I can't come back," I said.

"You don't have to."

I was glad Auntie LaRue understood. For the first time in my life, I was afraid of my mother. My throat started hurting because I was trying not to cry. My knees were knocking together, and I was squeezing my aunt's long bony hand so hard I was sure her bones were going to break. Auntie pried my hand off hers, and then she gently sat her hand on mine.

Finally, we said goodbye to Mama and watched as the attendants walked her back into the hospital. I was no longer able to hold back the tears.

"Now listen, girl—you can't be gettin' on the bus cryin' like that. Wipe your face and get ahold of yourself."

I wiped my eyes and nose with the embroidered hankie that Auntie Eula Mae had given me in Chicago. I found my voice as we walked down Forest Avenue to the bus stop. I was holding onto my aunt's hand again, but not so tightly.

"Auntie, what happened to Mama?" I asked as we waited for the bus. "She was doin' good in Haynesville. What happened to her?"

"I honestly don't know."

"Does mental illness run in our family? I don't want that to happen to me. You know what happened with Uncle Henry."

"I don't know, honey. I just pray that it goes no further. And I believe Mamie Lee is gone get better."

I had another flashback. I was back in the field, staring at Uncle Henry sprawled out on the ground. He had never been right; he had even liked Rosalie in an unnatural way. I hoped I was wrong, but I was scared to death that Mama was going to meet the same fate as Uncle Henry.

In spite of everything, I had to live my life. While I still wasn't crazy about my new hometown, summer wasn't so bad. Having never been to an amusement park, I thought the Crystal Beach amusement park in Canada had to be the best place in the world. I was amazed that we lived right next door to another country.

The park had a wooden roller coaster called the Comet. The roller coaster, with all its fast drops and turns, would have everyone screaming with delight. The rides and attractions were great, but I also loved the junk food—the cotton candy, suckers, french fries with vinegar and ketchup, sugar waffles, and the loganberry drinks.

Because Mama was in the hospital, Crystal Beach was a wonderful diversion for me that first summer in Buffalo. When I was there, for a few hours, I could forget about my mother's plight. Vivian and I would also walk downtown to go to a concert or to the movies.

Mama stayed in the hospital for three long years, and I'm ashamed to say that I never went back to see her. Vivian never once went to see her, and no one pressured her to do so. We would occasionally stay with other relatives during that period of time, but we mainly stayed with Auntie LaRue.

❖❖❖

By the time Mama was released from the hospital, I was pregnant. I wasn't particularly interested in boys because my mind was on my mother and trying to get an education. My dream was coming true; I was learning to make clothes, and my relatives had even bought me a used sewing machine. While not the smartest student, I managed to maintain passing grades.

I had met Myles Henderson while waiting in line for one of the rides at Crystal Beach. We would talk on the phone sometimes. He was just a boy. There was nothing special about him. We were both seventeen-year-old seniors. He attended East High School, and I attended Fosdick Masten High School.

Myles's skin was light brown, and his thick mustache and long sideburns gave him the appearance of a guy in his twenties. My heart didn't flutter, and my stomach didn't quiver when I was around Myles. Perhaps the appeal was that he was the first boy to ask me out on a date. We went to the movies one Saturday afternoon, and then we went a few more times.

On one of our dates, after the movie, we went to the park. Myles had borrowed his older brother's car. He drove to a deserted area of the park, and we started kissing. The next thing I knew, I was lying on my back in the back seat of the car. Myles flipped up my skirt, unzipped his pants, and we had sex with all our clothes on. I didn't enjoy one second of what we had done. It hurt more than anything.

After our intimate encounter, Myles Henderson disappeared from my life. He stopped calling and coming around. When I would call his house, he was never available. I was crushed, not because I liked him so much, but after all, I had lost my virginity to him. I didn't know that boys simply cut you off after the first encounter.

Myles wasn't thinking about me, but I had missed my cycle three months in a row. I was smart enough to know what that meant. I needed to talk to someone. Mama was out of the hospital, but she wasn't the person to talk to. She looked weak and thin and reminded me of my grandmother during her life in the backwoods, always staring at something that only she could see.

Auntie LaRue had taken Mama downtown to the welfare office so that she could have some income, and she spent most of her days sitting in front of the television in Aunt Bessie's parlor.

"She'll get her strength back, and the doctors said she should be fine," Auntie LaRue had said.

Auntie LaRue's upstairs apartment that Viv, Mama, and I shared in Aunt Bessie's house, was actually nothing more than one large bedroom. There was no kitchen or dining area, not even a toilet.

One night when Vivian and I were in the bed, I blurted out to her that I wasn't a virgin anymore. My mother was downstairs with my aunts, who were playing cards.

Vivian gasped. She sat up in bed, resting her back on the headboard.

She stared at me in disbelief. "Lilly, we are *not* supposed to be doin' that. You know Auntie told us we're not supposed to be havin' sex. And you remember what Auntie Eula Mae told Rosalie about havin' babies out of wedlock. It can sabotage your future."

"I already missed three periods."

Vivian gasped again. She looked hurt. "You have to tell Mama."

"I can't tell Mama. She's still sick."

"But she's gettin' better."

"*I can't tell Mama.*"

Vivian wasn't going to be able to change my mind. In her fragile condition, I didn't see how Mama could help me anyway. "Okay then, what about telling Auntie LaRue? She'll be able to help you."

I shook my head. "I'm too scared to tell anyone besides you." I looked at Vivian and asked, "How come you haven't asked me about the father?"

"Because I already know who it is. It's that sorry Myles Henderson. Right?"

"Yeah, it's him. Why you call him sorry?"

"Well, for one thing, he doesn't have any manners. Every time he came to get you, he blew the horn instead of comin' to the door like a gentleman. I just don't like him. Did you at least tell *him* that you're pregnant?"

"You're right. He *is* sorry. And no, I didn't tell him. Even if I did tell him, he wouldn't care."

"How do you know he wouldn't care?"

"Because we only *did it* one time, and I haven't seen him or talked to him since. Every time I call his house, the person who answers the phone tells me he's not home."

Vivian sucked her teeth. "You told me you had stopped talkin' to him."

"I did, because he stopped talkin' to me."

"He's avoidin' you. Dirty nigga. He's a cockroach. Somebody needs to smash him like the nasty bug he is. And you *need* to tell Mama or Auntie LaRue or *somebody*." Vivian's voice was rising.

"Hush," I said. "You're too loud."

"We're gonna tell Myles."

Vivian surprised me. She was being very mature. It was as though she was the older sister, and I was going to do what she told me to do.

My life was a mess. I didn't have a father, my mother was recovering from a breakdown, and I was always afraid that I was going to get sick like Mama did.

I didn't *really* have a home. My belly was beginning to protrude, which I tried to hide with larger blouses that I bought from the Goodwill. And I knew that Myles Henderson cared as much about me as he did about a hangnail.

Vivian insisted that Myles should know about the baby. So the next day after school, we caught the bus to his house. I was nervous and actually had not expected him to be home. But he answered the doorbell and stepped out onto the porch.

I got right to the point. "I'm havin' a baby."

"Your baby," Vivian chimed in.

He looked from me to Vivian, and then he leaned over the railing and spit in the grass. He turned around to go back into his house, without a word.

"Hey, where are you goin'?" Vivian asked. She grabbed his arm.

He jerked his arm away, giving my baby sister a hateful look. "I ain't got nothin' to do with no baby."

I couldn't believe how cold he was, and it made me angry. "It's *your* baby," I shouted. "I haven't been with any other boy."

He was almost grinning, and I was ready to fight. I balled my fists so tightly my nails made my palms feel like they were on fire. My jaws were locked as tightly as my hands. My instincts told me to punch him in the mouth. But I had never even been in a fight before, and the way Myles obviously felt about me, I didn't think he would have any problem punching me right back.

"Look," he said, pointing at me, "you take your little sister and get the hell off my porch and go back home to your crazy mama."

I was standing on his porch, but everything seemed surreal. I was having another one of my nightmares. When I awoke from the nightmare, my *real* world was going to be different. Myles was going to be kind, loving, understanding, and helpful. Most of all, he was going to take care of his child. It was okay that he wasn't interested in marrying me. Who wants to get married at seventeen anyway? But he definitely was going to take care of his baby.

I was jarred back to reality by Vivian's voice. "I'm gonna call the police on you," Vivian said.

Myles laughed. "Go ahead. Call the police. They can't force me to take care of no baby that ain't mine." Myles disappeared into his house, leaving us to stare at the closed door.

"Come on, Lilly." Vivian took my arm, and we started down the steps. "Let's go home. You don't need that cockroach."

Myles may have been a cockroach, but he was the father of my baby. I felt sick and hopeless. I was barely able to see through the tears clouding my eyes as we walked down the street to the bus stop. We discussed the possibility of me telling his parents, but I quickly dismissed that idea. I didn't know them. I only knew his older brother, and he didn't seem to be any nicer than Myles was. I figured the whole family must be like Myles, and I didn't think they would care about me having a baby.

I appreciated Vivian trying to help me, but I finally decided to go home and tell Auntie LaRue about my plight.

I didn't have a chance to tell my aunt anything. When we arrived home, all our Buffalo relatives were gathered in the house. Auntie LaRue walked over to us, put her arms around our shoulders, and whispered, "Mother died."

Vivian started crying. I had no tears, but I hugged my sister.

I didn't cry until the day of Mother's funeral, and then it was a flood of tears. I loved my quiet little grandmother. But I could hardly concentrate on her loss, as I was dealing with the biggest problem of my young life.

CHAPTER 7

※ ◆◆◆ ※

MOTHER WAS BURIED next to Uncle Henry and several other family members in the Negro cemetery in the Bottom. Poor Grandpa looked old and sad.

A bunch of us crowded into Uncle Slim's car, and he drove us to Georgia for the funeral. All of my grandparent's children and grandchildren came to bid Mother farewell, including Auntie Eula Mae, who flew in from Los Angeles along with Rosalie and Rhonda. The three had relocated to California after my aunt had divorced her husband.

I had come to appreciate Rosalie and was happy to see her. She had taught Vivian and me to read and write, which meant the world to me. Rosalie had met a nice young man and was engaged to be married.

At Mother's funeral, I honestly don't know if I cried more for myself or for her. I was a tortured soul. I still hadn't told an adult that I was pregnant. Being in Georgia just made me want to revert back to life on the pecan farm—to go back to being eleven or twelve. After all, I wasn't handling my teen years very well.

How could a few years have made such a difference, *for the worse*, in my life?

As soon as I saw Honey, I made the impulsive decision to tell her that I was pregnant. Time was moving, and I was going to go crazy if I didn't tell an adult. I needed someone to help me. Honey's little boy, Georgie, was getting big and was as cute as ever. When she finished scolding him for some little kid stuff that he was doing, I asked her if I could talk to her.

Honey helped me tell Mama that I was pregnant. My mother didn't have much of a reaction. She simply said that we would have to find a house of our own to live in because we couldn't bring a baby into her sister's house.

⸺ ◆◆◆ ⸺

I was back home from Mother's funeral, in the dark room, with only the dim glow of the streetlight outside to cause dark shadows. I was sprawled out on the bed. Blood was everywhere. The pain, though only in my mind, was so intense that I almost gagged. I lurched awake from a nightmare, bathed in a cold sweat. I was practically panting. My heart beat as though I'd run for five miles at top speed. I'd had strange dreams and panic attacks before. They scared me. After telling Mama about the baby, my next fear was delivering a child, and I was plagued by nightmares. I had never forgot how much pain Honey had been in when she was delivering her little boy.

I became obsessed with the thought of going back to Georgia to live; somehow I felt that relocation could remove me from the reality of my circumstances. I realized that I had no business having a baby.

With the help of the welfare department, Mama found an apartment and bought furniture and appliances for it. Vivian was still in school, but I had dropped out. Mama and I were in Auntie LaRue's room packing up our meager possessions for the move.

"Mama, do you think I can go back down south to live with Grandpa?" I asked.

Mama stopped folding her underwear, sat down on the bed, and stared at me like I was crazy. "You gonna go back to Georgia to live with Grandpa?" She snickered and shook her head in disbelief. "What do you wanna go down there for?"

"I miss living there," I said.

"*Girl, those days are over.* You about to have a baby, and Grandpa certainly can't help you with no baby."

I couldn't help it. I sat down on the bed and cried. Through sobs, I said, "I'm scared to have this baby, Mama." The anxiety that I felt was overwhelming. I wanted my mother to take me in her arms and tell me that everything was going to be all right.

Instead, she said, "Well, you should have thought about that before you opened your legs up for that boy." Mama was *definitely* coming back to life. She had even started wearing her wig again and painting her brown lips red.

My childhood had been left behind the minute I started worrying about becoming a mother, yet I certainly didn't feel like a grown woman. I was dangling between two worlds. I knew that being an adult was going to have to win out, though, because I would have a child to care for.

I was still holding out hope that Myles would miraculously appear at my door and want to be a part of his child's life. Myles was young, just as I was. But I couldn't wrap my mind around him not caring about the life that he had helped to create. I didn't understand why all the responsibility had to fall on me.

I did give it one last try with Myles. I went to a pay phone one afternoon after shopping for baby clothes at the Goodwill.

"I told you I'm not interested in no damn baby. Now leave me the hell alone and don't call my house no more." He hung up on me. I was devastated after that phone call, and I wished I had never laid eyes on Myles Henderson.

··· ❖❖❖ ···

Bridgett was born around one o'clock in the morning in October 1957. I delivered her after a long, hard labor at Kings Memorial Hospital, a hospital for unwed mothers. I felt as if I was drowning in a sea of loneliness when my baby came into the world. No one, including me, was happy or excited about her birth.

Bridgett weighed a little over five pounds, reminding me of my old Raggedy Ann doll. But she wasn't a doll. Instead of going back to school, because I needed to feed my child, I got a job. I didn't want to go on welfare because my mother was already getting assistance. Plus, I had heard that black women were given a hard time when they applied for assistance.

Auntie LaRue had a new suitor who was a preacher. He also owned a café on William Street. He hired me as a waitress. I was eighteen, and I felt like a grown-up with a job and the responsibility of a child.

··· ❖❖❖ ···

To celebrate my nineteenth birthday, I went to the Taps Room, a popular dance hall, with my friends Ruby and Wanda. We were sitting at a table tapping our toes, sipping on pop, and waiting for someone to come over and ask us to dance.

Suddenly, Mr. Beautiful appeared at our table. Mr. Beautiful had thick eyebrows and curly, black hair. "Hello ladies," he said. Then, extending his hand, he asked me to dance. I *had* to take his hand to steady myself so I wouldn't fall off my chair. This pretty man was asking *me* to dance!

I let him guide me to the crowded dance floor. The song was a slow jam, and I felt like I was in a dream. As we danced, he held me close but not too tightly.

"What's your name?" he breathed into my ear. He smelled like a fresh shower and musk cologne. "What's your name?" he asked again.

For a split second I'd truly forgotten my name, but I came back to my senses and told him.

"Nice to meet you, Lilly. I'm Walter."

Walter and I danced until the lights came on. I barely paid any attention to my friends the rest of the night. We met back up at the door, giggling like the silly girls that we were.

"Girl, you know he's fine, right? Did you give him your phone number?" Ruby asked. "Cause if you didn't, I'm gonna find him and give him *my* number."

We giggled some more.

"I didn't give him my number, but I told him where I work," I said as we walked outside to hail a cab.

⸺ ❖❖❖ ⸺

Walter showed up at my job the next day. He sat on a stool at the counter and ordered a sandwich and coffee.

I had outgrown my knees knocking when I was nervous, and this fine man *definitely* made me nervous. The knee knocking was replaced by a queasy feeling in my stomach.

I placed his order on the counter, and he asked, "How you doin' today, Lilly?"

Not only had he shown up at my job, but he had also remembered my name. I was outdone!

"I'm fine. How are you?" I responded.

"I'm doin' fine too."

⚬ ❖❖❖ ⚬

I convinced Mama to let me have Walter Davis over for dinner the following Sunday. And I did have to convince her because she wasn't the most trusting person; she scoped out strangers with a sharp, skeptical eye.

Once Mama warmed up to the idea, she agreed to prepare the meal. I wasn't a good cook, but Mama was a great cook. While I helped her prepare the meal, Vivian watched the baby.

We were renting the downstairs apartment from our landlord. He and his young family occupied the upstairs apartment. They were kind to us. Mrs. Jackson would occasionally watch Bridgett for me if Mama was doing day work in the homes of the wealthy people in North Buffalo.

Walter showed up at the house smelling as good as when I'd first met him, and he brought even more charm. He presented Mama, Vivian, and me with a fresh red rose each and brought a toy for the baby.

I felt special. Out of all the girls at the dance hall, Walter could have picked any one of them, and they probably would have been happy to be his girl. But he had picked *me*.

As a nineteen-year-old girl, it didn't take me long to fall in love with Walter Davis. Myles had been a mistake, although I did not feel that Bridgett was a mistake.

Walter, by contrast, was kind, generous, and attentive, to me as well as to my family. He took me downtown to shop for the baby because everything she owned was secondhand. I was beginning to think that my child would have a father after all. He was from New York City and was living in Buffalo with his sister. He was working at one of the plants, and he obviously was making good money.

One night after a trip to the dance hall, he asked me to come to his sister's house.

"Okay," I said, "but I can't stay long. I have to get back home to the baby."

"It's still early. I'll get you home at a decent hour."

"By midnight," I said.

"By midnight," he agreed.

Not only was I beginning to think my child would have a father, but maybe I would have a husband too. Up until that point, I hadn't thought too much about marriage. I wasn't one of those girls who had spent hours daydreaming about a knight in shining armor coming and whisking me away to a life of wedded bliss.

Walter unlocked the door to his sister's house and turned on the lights. "Where is everyone?" I asked.

"They all went down to New York to visit my mother."

"Why didn't you go?"

"I couldn't get the time off from work. Make yourself comfortable. I'll get us something to drink."

Walter came back from the kitchen with a bottle of wine and two glasses that he set on the coffee table. I wasn't a drinker, and I started to ask for a soft drink. But I wanted to please him. He took an album out of the jacket and put it on the record player. It was jazz. He took off his suit jacket, carefully laid it on the arm of the couch, and sat down close to me. His thigh touched mine, and then the butterflies started.

The wine relaxed me. I was nervous about being alone with Walter for the first time since I'd known him. I was feeling a buzz and relaxed in his arms as we began to kiss. It was too late to run home to my baby. He kissed my lips, my forehead, and my neck. Before I knew it, I was following Walter into his bedroom.

Walter was a hard man to resist. The musk cologne, the wine, the kissing and petting—it was all intoxicating. We sat on the bed and slowly undressed. His gentle kisses found every tender spot on my body. I wanted to hold Walter tight and stay with him all night, but I had a baby to get home to. I told him so.

Ignoring my weak protesting, he laid me down gently and got on top of me. "Your mama and sister are taking care of your little girl just fine," he said, his hot breath on my ear. Being with Walter took me to a place where I never wanted to leave. But I was worried about what Mama would say about my being out so late. So after we made love, I had Walter take me home.

When I got there, Mama was waiting up for me. She said, "You be careful with that man, Lil. You don't want to bring no more babies home."

Auntie LaRue also tried to caution me against getting too involved with Walter. "You're too young, Lilly. You have all the time in the world to settle down with a man, and you don't want to get caught with another baby. You need to think more about your future."

I ignored my mother's and aunt's admonishments. They were old. What did they know?

From that point on, for weeks, I spent all my free time with Walter, to the exclusion of everyone except Bridgett. I would take the baby with me to Walter's sister's house to play with her little kids.

And I got pregnant again.

When I told Walter that I was having a baby, he turned as cold as a block of ice.

Walter had become one of my main reasons for living, but his response to my news was that he had a wife and young daughter back home in New York City. "I'm just working here temporarily, and then I'm goin' back home to my family."

What?! What family? I thought we were going to be a family.

It was late in the evening, and Walter had just picked me up from work. We were still sitting outside of the café, in his car, while this conversation was going on.

I had been so excited to tell him the news. I'd spent the day fantasizing about how things would be after I had told Walter about the baby. I was so sure that he'd pick me up and give me a big kiss. We would start making plans to get married.

Instead, he told me about his family, and I became sick to my stomach. Dizzy and nauseous, I threw up my dinner. I tried to hold the vomit, but I couldn't get the door open fast enough, and I threw up on the floor of the car. My dinner landed on his shiny black leather shoes.

Disgusted, Walter got out of the car in a huff, walked around to the passenger side, opened the door, and ordered me out.

Barely coherent, I said "What?"

"I said get out … Throwin' up in my damn car." He grabbed my arm and pulled me out of the car. He pushed me away from the car, and with tires screeching, he sped off.

Standing on the sidewalk in front of the diner, I could see the patrons sitting at the Formica tables, eating the soul food that Harold, the cook, had become famous for. Less than an hour earlier, I had been in the diner serving food and eagerly anticipating seeing the love of my life so that I could tell him about our baby.

Now I was standing in the cold November air, feeling as lost as a five-year-old separated from her mother in Central Park. I didn't know what to do, so I stumbled back into the diner and went to the kitchen where Bill was cleaning dishes. I was crying when I asked him if he could give me a ride home.

"What's wrong?" he asked, looking at me with his hands still in the dishwater.

"I need a ride home, please. My ride left me."

I didn't feel comfortable telling Bill my troubles, so I was quiet while he drove me home. When he pulled up to the house, I thanked him for the ride and told him that I would see him tomorrow.

Slowly I walked up the stairs and unlocked the door. Mama was sitting on the couch in the living room, watching television. I wasn't ready to face my mother, to tell her that I had messed up again. I needed time to process the scene that had just taken place between Walter and me.

Mama said that Bridgett was asleep, so I told her I was tired and was going to bed. I cried myself to sleep that night. In the morning, before Vivian went to school, I told her that I was pregnant.

It was March 1959. African Americans were in the midst of the struggle for justice, and I was struggling to make sense out of my life. Once again, I found myself crying on Vivian's shoulder. I believed that Vivian had way more sense than I did. She had quit high school in her senior year, just as I had done, and was doing day work and babysitting. But at least she wasn't messing her life up by fooling around with men who would love you and leave you. Vivian said she wanted to get her driver's license and become a city bus driver.

My sister took charge, just as she had done in my first pregnancy. She decided that we should go to Walter's job because, just as Myles had done, Walter made himself scarce.

Humble, contrite, and feeling like a fool, I conceded, albeit much too late, that Mama and my aunt had indeed known what was best for me.

When Walter finally came outside, he had a scowl on his face, but he didn't say anything. I broke the silence. Nervously, but with hope, I said, "Walter, why are you actin' like this? This is your baby, and you know I need help." I practically screamed the word *help*. I was scared. I didn't want to have another child to support on my own. I certainly didn't want to bring another child home for my mother to have to help me with, especially after I had ignored her admonishments about Walter.

"I never said it wasn't my baby, but what you need to do is get an abortion. I already told you I'm married and I'm goin' back to my wife."

With the foreign word "abortion" still ringing in my ear, he snatched his work glove off his left hand. A gold wedding band circled his finger. "Now make this the last time you come to my job bothering me. You got that?" He hissed the word *last*, making it sound like a threat.

He was the devil! I was convinced that Walter had turned into the devil right before my eyes. He walked back through the doors of the plant, and I fell into my sister's arms, sobbing.

Vivian took the pink hankie from her purse that she still had from our trip to Chicago. She dabbed my eyes and brushed my cheeks with the hankie. *What would I do without this girl?* I wondered.

Hand in hand, we silently walked to the bus stop.

I stared out the window the whole ride home. Rosalie's words came clearly to my mind. *It will sabotage your future.* I had since learned what the word meant, and it was exactly what I was doing to myself. I was sabotaging my own future. On that sad bus ride home, I resolved that I was never again going to sleep with another man who was not my husband.

Then I got the bright idea to talk to Walter's sister. Surely she would be able to talk some sense into her brother's head.

Beverly resembled her younger brother. Her skin was a flawless caramel color, and she had those thick eyebrows, although hers were nicely shaped. We sat at the table in her brightly colored kitchen. She liked apples, and they were everywhere—the print on the wallpaper, the curtains, and fresh ones in a bowl on the counter. She wore an apron decorated with red apples. Her three small children were down for a nap, and her husband was at work.

Beverly was the picture of domestic tranquility. My life was in turmoil, and I yearned for what she had. Oh, the contrast! How could she have such a brother?

Beverly offered me a cup of tea, and we sat at her kitchen table. "How could Walter change on me like that? I don't understand. It's like he's two different people." My bottom lip was quivering, and I was about to cry more useless tears, but I was tired of crying.

His sister was a nice woman, but she was blunt with me. "I know that he and his wife were having problems. I told him he was running away from his responsibilities by coming here to work. His job transferred him here on a temporary basis, but I told him he should have stayed home. Anyway, he was sending Michelle money. But he insisted that he was going to get a divorce."

Michelle. Hearing his wife's name brought on the tears. Beverly handed me tissues, and I wiped my eyes and nose.

"The only reason I could be halfway decent to you is because he said he was getting a divorce. I didn't like the fact that he was seeing you while his wife was in New York. I don't know if she knew about you." Beverly paused and shook her head. Then she said, "You're too young for him anyway."

So I felt like a useless piece of trash. "He didn't tell me that he was going back to his wife. Well, actually, he didn't even tell me he was married until the night I told him I was pregnant."

Beverly reached across the table and put her hand on mine. "I'm sorry for all this, Lilly. I did talk to him, but he got mad and left. He's back home now."

I put my forehead down on her kitchen table and sobbed, my chest heaving. Walter was back with his beloved family, and I was left to take care of the baby that he didn't want.

I lifted my head up, gained control of myself, and wiped my face with more tissues.

Beverly looked at me with pity. "Lilly, I wanna tell you something that I've learned about relationships. Women ... girls need love. We're built that way. I believe God means for us to be loved. Men need respect and sex. Women need love and affection. I know that you haven't had a father in your life to teach you how a man should treat you. And I believe you've been looking for love, Lilly, just the wrong way."

No one had ever told me those things before, but I nodded my head in agreement because she was making sense.

"So if you believe what I'm saying is correct, then my advice would be, going forward, be very, very careful about who you get involved with. Go slow. You're gonna need to be cautious anyway because you have children to consider."

I took Beverly's advice as words of wisdom. Sitting at her kitchen table made me realize how ignorant I had been. I had never gotten the guidance that a young girl needed. When I was first menstruating, I'd had no idea why I was bleeding. I remember being frightened and dumbfounded. *What was going on?* I had wrapped my blood-soaked underwear in newspaper and thrown them in the trash. That same evening, at dinner, I found myself sitting in a pool of blood. Mother gathered some rags for me to stuff in my underwear and helped me to clean up the mess.

Mother had given me plenty of rags for the next six days, but she didn't tell me why I was bleeding, and I didn't have the good sense to ask. I was never told anything about sex. Now I was learning my lessons the hard way. That's why Beverly's words weren't offensive to me. I had not been smart, but I would be going forward.

"If I can help you with anything, let me know. I do have some baby things that I can give you, if you want them."

"Yes. Thank you," I said and left Beverly's home.

On the bus ride home, I thought about what she had told me about relationships. I *definitely* had been looking for love, maybe a father's love. But in the process, I may as well have stepped into quicksand.

I cried myself to sleep that night, and then I got on with my life. I had no other choice.

••• ❖❖❖ •••

About five months later, I went into labor. I knew all the signs. I was ready this time. When the doctor handed me my second daughter, it was all I could do not to cry. "Jewel," I said. "I'm gonna call her Jewel."

Jewel, a beautiful baby, came into the world in April 1959. When the nurses demonstrated bathing the newborns in the hospital, they used my baby. She was beautiful and precious, but I had mixed emotions about her and contemplated putting her up for adoption. I had nothing to offer her. I was a high school dropout living with my mother, my sister, and my toddler.

Mama talked me out of surrendering Jewel for adoption. "How you gone feel if you never see her again or if you don't know where she is?"

Mama asked me that while I was sitting in the hospital bed holding Jewel. My tears fell on her face. I wiped them away and decided that I couldn't do it.

I've heard that there were drastic differences in how black and white families treated their daughters who became pregnant out of wedlock. Whereas with many white families the young woman was banished to a home for unwed mothers until the child was born and then often put up for adoption; in the black community there wasn't a big stigma attached to not being married. In fact, just as my mother had done with me, adoption was discouraged.

Although I wasn't shunned by my family, I knew that having another child was the last thing I needed to be doing. So I was miserable and did a pretty good job of beating myself up. I brought my baby home, and visions of murder and suicide began to occupy my head. I was consumed with the desire to find Walter Davis and murder him. I wanted to take a brick and shatter all his car windows. The thoughts were ever present. I could be changing the baby's diaper or giving her a bath, but my mind would be on violence.

One day, while I was dressing Jewel after a bath, I started crying and praying. I asked God to take those destructive thoughts from me because I was afraid I was going to act on them. I had gone to church enough to know that I needed deliverance from the evil thoughts that I couldn't seem to control.

"Please, God. Help me to forget about Walter Davis. And help me to take care of these kids." I knew I needed a miracle to forget about him while caring for his child every day. I promised God that if he would help me, I wouldn't have any more children out of wedlock. The prayer did seem to help, as my desire to kill Walter subsided and, in time, went away.

But life was a struggle. My babies and I slept in the same room. As promised, Beverly brought me her daughter's baby clothes, and her husband dropped off a white wooden cradle. Before the cradle, I had made a bed for Jewel from one of my dresser drawers.

The community may not have scorned me for my poor choices, but welfare was another matter. The women who sat smugly behind the desks at the welfare office, charged with doling out assistance, gave me a hard time when I applied for the relatively small amount of money they provided.

The welfare office wanted to collect support from the fathers. I gave them what information I had, but I'm not aware of them ever getting any money from either man. With welfare barely giving me enough money to live on, when Jewel was around two months old, I took an overnight job cleaning offices in a bank. That work shift worked well, as it enabled Mama and Vivian to watch the kids with the least amount of disruption to their lives.

A few months after being on the job, I was invited by a young man to go roller-skating, and I gladly went. I considered Barry a friend, but I didn't think of our outing as a real date. Neither of us had a car, and we both lived near the skating rink, so we walked.

We met some friends there, and we hung out with them. I fell on my behind a couple of times, but we had fun. When we left and were walking home, Barry suddenly grabbed my arm and threw me up against a building. Then he started groping me.

We tussled. "What are you doing? What is wrong with you?" I was screaming and hitting him upside the head with my purse. "Are you crazy?!"

"Aw, girl, come on. You know you want it. You ain't no virgin. You already got two kids. I thought maybe you wanted one more."

"I don't want nothing," I yelled. "And I thought you were my friend." I loosed myself from his clutches. "You stay away from me, or I'll have you arrested," I said, and I ran all the way home.

The next day, I told Ruby what had happened. Ruby had one little boy, and she lived with her parents. She said, "When you have kids and no husband, men think you're fast and easy."

"I'm not fast, and I'm not easy. I was just ignorant." I was feeling quite defensive.

I immediately decided that not only was I swearing off premarital sex, I wasn't dating anymore. I didn't hate men, and I knew there were good men in the world. But for me, men meant trouble. I didn't need any more of them or their trouble. I decided to take care of my children and leave the other half of the human race alone.

CHAPTER **8**

❖❖❖

THE YEARS PASSED quickly. I had gone back to school to get my LPN diploma and was working at Memorial Hospital. My girls were growing and doing well in school. The country moved into the tumultuous 1960s, with the Vietnam War and war protests raging.

For us, 1965 was a particularly remarkable year. Grandpa, elderly, frail, and with much protest, moved to Buffalo to live with Aunt Bessie and Uncle Slim. Suffering from dementia, sadly, he lived out his last days in the same facility that Mama had been in after her nervous breakdown.

Riots broke out. It was a frightening time. Mama and I called Rosalie and Auntie Eula Mae to check on them because they lived in Watts, which was experiencing riots. They were fine, but dozens of people were dying.

My days were spent working in the burn treatment unit of the hospital. The evenings were spent getting dinner for the girls; making sure they did their homework; and, when I wasn't too tired after that, designing and making clothes.

Celeste Hall, a friend from work, had been asking me to come for dinner at her house. She was newly married to a musician, Mike, and she wanted me to meet his friend, a fellow musician. Every time she asked, I declined.

Celeste was petite and possessed a gentle manner, which was perfect for anxious patients and their families. She was one of only two black RNs at the hospital. We had become friends as we worked together in the burn unit.

Celeste persisted in trying to convince me to meet her husband's friend. One day, when our seven-to-three shift was over and we were leaving the building, she said, "Lil, you know, we're supposed to learn from our mistakes, not punish ourselves for them."

I walked with Celeste to her car, and we leaned against it. It had been seven years since my relationship with Walter Davis. Sadly, neither of my girls knew who her father was. I maintained that the only thing a man could do for me was step aside so I could pass by. But in my quiet time, after the girls were asleep and it was just me and my sewing machine, I had to admit that I was lonely.

Celeste was a persistent soul. "Lilly, you know, men are people too. They have feelings also. And they're not *all* bad."

"Did you tell this guy about me? I mean, does he know that I have kids?"

"Yes. I told him that you have two beautiful little girls, and I told him that their mother is gorgeous."

I snickered.

"Come on, Lilly," Celeste said. "It's just a dinner, not a lifetime commitment."

"Okay. Okay."

Celeste's face lit up, and she gave me a quick hug. "Okay, I'll let you know tomorrow what day I set up. I'm so excited. You want a ride home?" she asked as she got into her car.

"No, thank you. I'll see you tomorrow." I walked home, wondering what I was getting myself into.

Trying to decide what to wear to Celeste's house for dinner, just about every piece of clothing I owned was in a heap on my bed. When I finally emerged from my bedroom in a peach dress, with matching heels, Jewel told me I looked pretty. My sixteen-year-old neighbor came over to watch the girls.

"You look great," Celeste said when she picked me up.

"I just hope I don't make a fool of myself," I said as we pulled up to her house.

Celeste was a newlywed and very enthusiastic about marriage. "Seven years of singleness is long enough. Dating with the right person is fun. Maybe Wells is the right person."

I got cold feet and didn't want to get out of the car. "Celeste, I have an anxiety problem, and I don't need to be dating anyone."

My friend put her hand on mine. "Lil, it's just dinner, and he really is a nice guy. So please try to relax and enjoy yourself."

Celeste's husband, Mike, and Weldon McClendon, whose nickname was Wells, were sitting in the living room talking. When we walked in, they rose from the couch. Wells was a head taller than Mike, who was not a short man.

Wells drove a cab during the week and played in the band two weekends per month. He was a full-time college student on the GI Bill. He stepped forward and enveloped my small hand into his large dark one. "Very nice to meet you, Lilly," he said.

As we ate dinner, I said very little. But I caught Wells eyeing me several times. He talked about his experience being drafted into the Vietnam War and serving as a US Marine. I detested violence and didn't understand war.

"It was hell," Wells, who had been shot in the shoulder, said. "I was one of the lucky ones. The majority of the guys in my platoon were gravely injured, and more than half of them died."

I shuddered. How could he talk so casually and seem so normal after experiencing what the average person couldn't even imagine?

"How about a game of rummy?" Mike said, after we finished eating. Mike had escaped serving in the war because of asthma.

When the evening was over, Wells offered to give me a ride home. I didn't want to get into the car with a stranger, but Celeste would never put me in harm's way, so I accepted the ride.

Wells walked me to my apartment door and told me he had really enjoyed spending the evening with me. "How about you come to the club next Friday night to hear the band?" he asked.

He had been a gentleman and seemed to be a nice person. "Okay, sure," I said. "That sounds nice."

*** ❖❖❖ ***

The club where Wells and his band played every other weekend was not big enough for the crowd. Every table and seat in the smoky, dark place was filled. The bar was crowded, and the atmosphere was something I'd never experienced before. I knew when I walked into the Palmaire Room that something special was going on. I had heard about the club, but I did not go out much and had never been there before.

All eyes were on the center of the stage, where Wells's long torso leaned in, strumming his acoustic guitar. Mike Hall's hands were making magic with his electric guitar. And in the middle of the two men was a young woman about my age. She was brown-skinned and heavily made up, but I could tell there was beauty underneath all that paint. She wore a white top, a pink leather miniskirt, pink fishnet stockings, and white go-go boots. The trio was doing a Sam Cooke song in perfect harmony. And then the lady sang a song that I wasn't familiar with, but she had a voice that was hypnotizing, crescendoing from one octave to the next. Glass should have shattered.

The night was thrilling. I was a music lover, though I couldn't hold a note and had absolutely no rhythm. The band took a break. Wells; Mike; and the female singer, Zena James, found some chairs and sat down at our table.

The trio ordered drinks; Wells's was a soda, and I remembered him telling me that he was a teetotaler, something we had in common.

"You have a beautiful voice, Zena," I said, shouting over the noise.

"Thank you. But I can't take any credit for it. It's a gift from God."

I nodded in agreement and said, "You all sound great together."

When the group reconvened on the stage, Celeste said, "Isn't this awesome? Aren't you glad you came?"

"Actually I am. I'm having a great time."

The next morning, which was Saturday, my phone rang. It was Wells calling. He said, "My mother taught me that unless it's an emergency, never call anyone before 9:00 a.m."

"So what's the emergency?" I asked, looking at the clock.

"I need to take you to lunch this afternoon."

I laughed.

"Okay. Good. That's a yes," he said in response to my yes. "Dress up because we're going to a fancy restaurant."

I was familiar with pretty much every place on our side of town, and I wouldn't have called any of them "fancy."

Wells took me to the Remington. His brother worked there as the sous chef. The Remington was where a lot of the big stars who came to town ate after a performance.

Wells had made reservations, and the maître d' politely seated us. I wore a beige pantsuit that I had recently bought, and Wells wore slacks and a suit jacket.

I was nervous about being one-on-one with Wells, and I had never been in such a nice restaurant before. I hoped I could enjoy my meal.

"Are you married?" I asked Wells.

He laughed softly. "No."

"Do you have a girlfriend?"

"No. I don't have anyone waiting for me at home. I wouldn't do something like that." Wells busied himself with cutting his steak into bite-size pieces. Then he looked at me and told me that I was a very beautiful lady.

I didn't even know how to take a compliment. I rolled my eyes. No one had ever called me *beautiful* before. In fact, as a child, my family members had felt it their duty to remind me that I was the ugly duckling of the family. But instead of arguing with him, I thanked him for the compliment.

We talked about the South. In 1964, the year before I met Wells, Lyndon Johnson had signed the Civil Rights Act into law, abolishing the Jim Crow laws that had mandated facilities be "separate but equal." Nothing was *equal,* and Jim Crow was simply a legally sanctioned method of brutally oppressing a group of people to keep them in a subservient position. Under Jim Crow, whites made a sport of lynching black people, including women and children.

Wells had been born in South Carolina, and his father had moved the family to Buffalo when he was a little boy because he'd feared for their lives and sought better opportunities. Wells was a tall, very dark young man, just the type who would have had a target on his back and would have had to kowtow to whites. He would have been called *darkie* all the time. Yet, he was so self-assured. He was different from any other man I'd known.

I, on the other hand, was a light-skinned woman and not at all threatening, even to the whites down south. But I suffered from low self-esteem, due in part, I'm sure, to the indignities that my family had suffered in Georgia. It saddens me even now to think how black people were so grossly mistreated simply because of the color of our skin.

"From the time we were little boys, my dad taught my brother and me that we're not better than anyone, but no one's better than we are either. And it's a good thing my dad got us out of the south when he did because I'm not the type to let someone call me a darkie and get away with it."

Wells swallowed some food and then said, "Hopefully things will get better. As far as you're concerned, Lilly, you're special. Remember that."

I was fascinated by and envious of Wells; he defied all my notions of how a young black man in America should be. He had an ease about him that I hoped would rub off on me.

Wells asked about my girls, who were with my mother. He wanted to know what they were like and if I had any pictures. When I pulled out my wallet and showed him a school portrait, he told me they were beautiful girls just like their mother. *He's so nice*, I said to myself.

After a few more dates, I decided that it was time for Wells to meet Bridgett and Jewel. I was nervous about bringing a new man into their lives. Wells figured the best way to get to know them was by doing something they liked to do. I had them dress in cute outfits, told them to be on their best behavior, and we all went roller-skating. After skating, we went back to my apartment for a fries and hamburger dinner.

The day was a lot of fun, and Wells was a hit with the girls. After he went home, Bridgett said she really liked Wells and asked if we were going to get married.

"No," I said, laughing.

To this day, Bridgett speaks fondly of Wells. She recalls things about him in vivid detail and refers to him as *daddy*. All these years later, she still has his driver's license and Marine dog tag. Jewel, on the other hand, barely remembers Wells and refers to him by his given name.

After Wells had me and the girls over to his parents' house for dinner, I knew that we were officially a couple, and it felt good. I felt comfortable and safe with Wells and not as anxious as I usually felt. I thought Celeste would be pleased to know her hookup was going well, so I gave her a call.

She was ecstatic. "See. Life is better with a good man. But watch out for Zena. She's a man-eater."

"A man-eater? What are you talking about, Celeste?"

"A *home-wrecker*, honey. Listen—I know for a fact that Zena will smile in your face and take your husband behind your back. And she's always liked Wells, although he's never been interested in her. So you just keep both eyes wide open."

"But we're not married," I said. I realize now how naive I sounded.

"Boyfriend or husband, it's all the same to Zena. Just watch out for her."

"Okay. Thanks for the heads-up. I'll talk to you later, Celeste."

Great, I thought, *just what I want to be bothered with ... a man-eating home-wrecker!*

••• ❖❖❖ •••

One evening, Wells came over after his shift driving the cab was over. He and I were sitting on the couch watching television. His long arm was draped around my shoulder. He said softly, "I love you, Lilly. Let's get married."

I had lain awake many nights since meeting Wells. I couldn't get him out of my mind. He was a year younger than me, but he was very mature. He said that being in the jungle, killing people, and watching his mates be mortally wounded had matured him.

Before the war, he had never had a white person as a friend. Our country was in turmoil. Whereas, at home, black people and white people weren't getting along, in war, blacks and whites became friends because the Vietnam War was the first fully integrated war. Wells matured as he saw a drastically different side of life, in a drastically different part of the world.

Consequently, he knew what he wanted from life. He planned to become a school guidance counselor so he could steer young people, especially disadvantaged black boys, into a better future. He wanted a nice home, and he wanted a family.

Through tears, I said, "Wells, you're the first person to ever tell me you love me."

Even though I knew Mama loved me, she had never told me so. Being enveloped in the embrace of Wells's love had me thinking about love and my family. *Love* hadn't been a word that was ever used in our family. Grandpa was duty bound, but I don't know if he loved anyone, including his wife.

Wasn't love as natural, as necessary as breathing? If so, why was it so elusive? And so complicated? Why was it easier to yell and scream or neglect or create war? What was lacking in human beings? Why did I have to wait until I was twenty-six years old before anyone told me they loved me?

Bridgett and Jewel had never heard the words *I love you* pass through my lips. I clothed them, fed them, and protected them like a mother hen protecting her chicks, but I had never uttered those three words. That night, I promised myself to start telling them I loved them. I would practice until it felt as natural as breathing.

To Wells's declaration of love and desire to get married, I said, "But we've only known each other for six months."

"So? What else is there to know? I know you. You know me. I love you. You love me. What else is there to this thing?"

"How you know I love you? I never told you that."

He removed his arm from around my shoulder and scooted away from me a little bit. "Lilly, I know you better than you think. I know that if you weren't completely comfortable with me, there is no way I would be sitting in this apartment with your little girls asleep in the other room. And I know that you love me; otherwise, you wouldn't be bothered with me. I know you, Lilly Brown."

I laughed. "I do love you, Wells. But what about Zena?"

Wells frowned. "Where's this comin' from? Why are you asking me about Zena?"

"Because I know she likes you, and Celeste told me she's a man-eater."

Wells cracked up laughing. "Listen. I've known that girl since I was thirteen years old. We've never been anything more than friends. Period. This is about you and me. So will you marry me?"

"I don't know, Wells. I don't want any surprises."

"Baby, you can trust me."

We kissed, and then I said, "Yes, Wells. I love you, and I'll be happy to marry you."

Wells took a small box from his pocket. He opened the box and showed me an oval-shaped diamond ring. He said, "So, if a girl's getting married, she should have a ring, right?"

"Yes, she should," I agreed, extending my hand so he could put the ring on my finger. "We're engaged," I said.

"You like the ring?"

"I love it." I could hardly believe that something so good was happening to me. Even though there was chaos going on in the world, it seemed as though things were being set right in my life, and I thanked God.

"I'll be a good husband for you and a good father for your girls. I promise."

With those words, I couldn't help but tear up.

"We're gonna buy a nice house after I graduate and get a job," Wells said.

I couldn't wait to wake up with him every morning, to fix his breakfast, and to see him off to the start of his days.

As I said before, I'd never had any girlish fantasies about getting married to a knight in shining armor and living happily ever after. Maybe that was because I hadn't seen many happily married couples. I had seen arranged unions like the brief one between my mother and Mr. Rooster and even Auntie LaRue and her pen pal turned husband. No, I hadn't known too many examples of marital bliss. But I went into my marriage to Wells believing the best.

Celeste was proud as a peacock at the successful matchmaking outcome. We had a nice wedding and reception at Wells's parents' house. After the reception, Wells and I spent a romantic weekend in Toronto. When we picked the girls up from my mother's apartment, Bridgett wanted to know if she and Jewel could call Wells *Daddy.*

"Yes," he said. "I'm Daddy now."

I came home from work one afternoon to find Wells and the girls sitting cross-legged on the floor. Wells was playing his guitar, Jewel was playing her plastic flute, and Bridgett was strumming the inexpensive starter acoustic guitar that he had bought for her.

They were singing "Frere Jacques," a song the girls had learned in school. Bridgett had already told me she wanted to be a singer when she grew up. It warmed my heart to see the three of them bonding so well.

CHAPTER 9

⬥ ⬥ ⬥

I HAD BEEN struggling with anxiety for years, and although things were going fairly well in my life, I still couldn't shake the anxiety. I occasionally called in sick from work because work was where I felt the most anxious. I had a fear of people, and I feared having a breakdown in front of them. I envisioned myself yelling and screaming, being forced into a straitjacket, and then carted away to the mental hospital.

Finally, one evening, unable to keep the problem to myself any longer, I confided in Wells. I thought he would be shocked or alarmed. But he had taken psychology courses in college and told me that my anxiety wasn't surprising to him, considering my family history.

He told me I needed to get some help.

"What kind of help?" I asked.

"There's a community mental health clinic that you can go to. If you make an appointment, I'll go with you."

I cried from the very thought of getting some relief, but I told Wells that I could go alone.

I was nervous and didn't know what to expect when I entered the psychiatrist's second-floor downtown office. The receptionist had me fill out paperwork, and I sat wringing my hands while awaiting the doctor. To my surprise, the doctor was a woman. She was middle-aged and plump and had long graying hair. When I walked into her office, her demeanor put me at ease, and I was able to tell her my symptoms and give her a brief life history.

"What do you think is your major problem?" she asked.

"I have an issue with control. I want to be in control of everything because, as a child, it seems that no one in my life had any control of their circumstances."

"What's your greatest fear?"

"Losing control at work, having a breakdown, and being committed to a mental institution."

"Who do you confide in?"

"My husband. He's the one who suggested I get help. But I don't like to bother him."

"It sounds like your husband loves you. As you go through this process, let him help you, okay?"

I nodded.

At the end of the session, the doctor handed me a prescription for antianxiety medication and told me to make a one-week follow-up appointment. I foolishly stopped going to counseling after two sessions. I told Wells that I didn't have time for it. I had to work, take care of the home, and take sewing lessons. The truth was that I was uncomfortable sharing my problems with a stranger, and I didn't think that counseling would help.

Wells was furious with me for quitting the counseling. We had our first big argument because of it. "What's more important to you, your sanity or making a shirt?"

"It's not just making a shirt. It's my dream. It's what I've wanted to do since I was nine years old."

"Well, I can't force you to go back to the counseling, but I want you to. What affects you affects all of us."

I wasn't comfortable with counseling, and I couldn't force myself to go, not even to please my husband. So I continued on as I had for years, with my good moments and bad moments. But I felt as though I had sown a seed of discord in my marriage by not continuing the counseling.

••• ❖❖❖ •••

We moved into an apartment in the Hamilton Mall projects. I got pregnant right away, so needing more space, we moved about a mile away to a four-bedroom apartment in the Tennyson Mall housing projects.

Both housing complexes were constructed at the same time, in 1959.

Thirty city blocks of what had previously been a racially mixed area were all demolished. Thousands of residents had been displaced. And when the complexes were completed, the population became almost completely black.

When we moved in, I didn't care how the projects had come to be. I felt like I was inhabiting a small slice of paradise. The buildings and grounds were clean and well cared for.

We lived at 219 South Street, on the eighth floor, the final floor of the building. The apartment had four bedrooms, two each on either side of a long hallway. There was a decent-sized dining room and living room. A large picture window gave us a view of life in the projects. We could look down and see guys playing basketball in the large, fenced-in basketball court. I could watch my kids enjoy themselves in the playground. The narrow, rectangle-shaped kitchen was the smallest room in the apartment and barely large enough for three people to occupy at the same time. The grocery store and barbershop were right across the street.

My apartment was high enough that the cars in the parking lot looked like toys that I could pick up between my forefinger and thumb. And our birds-eye view allowed Bridgett and Jewel to see Auntie LaRue when she was coming.

My aunt had taken care of Vivian and me as kids, so she felt it her duty to help out with my kids when I needed her. She'd be marching up to the building, purse strap dangling from her wrist, with the serious look of a drill sergeant.

The kids would scatter when they saw Auntie LaRue coming. They would run to their rooms to make sure everything was straightened up. When Mama and Auntie were around, they made sure the kids walked the straight and narrow.

Wells took care of Bridgett and Jewel as if they belonged to him. The central library was downtown. He took the girls to get library cards and emphasized to them that smart girls read *a lot*.

Wells and the band were still going strong on the weekends, and he was in his last year of college. Zena and I had become friendly. When she found out that I was a seamstress, she asked me to make a couple of maxi dresses for her.

Zena came to the apartment so we could firm up her clothing designs. She was about my height but quite a bit larger in the bust and derriere.

Though she wanted maxi dresses, she requested they have a side slit past the knee, and low cut in the front. She was partial to bold colors and paisley patterns.

"Lil, I'm tryin' to convince your husband to go into the studio with me so I can get this album recorded. I want to send a demo to a record company. I don't want to have to hire someone. I'm comfortable with Wells. I mean, I've been singing with him off and on since high school."

I could feel Zena's frustration. She was talking to me as I was taking her measurements. "Zena, Wells and I have had this conversation several times. He decided that he can't commit any more time to the music because of his other commitments. His time is already stretched to the limit."

"But, Lil, I know this record is gonna be a hit. And that means money and the big time."

"He's aware of all that. But he's married now, Zena. Everything's different. He doesn't want to be on the road touring. He has a family now. And he has every intention of using his college degree."

Zena left abruptly—but not before telling me that Wells was wasting his talent and time with a ready-made family. She slammed the door, and I suspected she had been talking to Wells's mother. I knew then that I wouldn't be making any more clothes for her.

⚜ ❖❖❖ ⚜

I was miserable working in the burn unit. Many of the area's critically injured patients came through our doors because they'd sustained devastating injuries, mainly from house fires. One poor little boy's penis had burned off. My plan was to ask for a transfer so that I would be able to work on a different unit after my baby was born.

Wells and I had been married around two years. Halfway through my shift one afternoon, the nursing supervisor, Mrs. Sands, summoned me to her office. I panicked. What mistake had I made that was serious enough for the supervisor to single me out? When I arrived at her office, she was standing by her desk with a grave look on her face. She was holding the phone.

"Have a seat, Lilly."

I knew I wasn't in trouble because her voice was too gentle. Choosing not to sit, I asked what was wrong.

"Lilly, this is Dr. Carr on the phone. He's from the veterans hospital, and he needs to talk to you about your husband."

In the middle of my conversation with the doctor, I threw down the receiver. Screaming, and although heavy from pregnancy, I started running down the hospital hallway. I guess my intention was to run all the way to the VA hospital. But Mrs. Sand was running after me, calling for me to stop.

"Lilly. Stop. What's happened to your husband?"

"I have to get to the hospital. The doctor said my husband's chest was crushed in a collision with a delivery truck. He's in ICU. The doctor said they're doing everything possible to save his life. I have to get to the hospital."

"Okay. I'll drive you. Just let me go back to my office to get my keys."

"I'll wait for you outside," I said. I needed to breathe in the frigid February air. I was crying, and my heart was pounding.

While my supervisor drove me to the hospital, I collected myself enough to write down names and numbers of the people who she had kindly offered to contact for me. Those people were my mother, my friend Peggy, and Wells's parents. I didn't want Celeste to know just yet because I knew how devastated she would be.

My heart was pounding again as Mrs. Sands and I hurried through the doors of the VA hospital. I'd never been there before that day, the first of many agonizing days over a period of weeks.

Dr. Carr talked to us. He needed me to know that my husband was in grave condition, but there was a chance he would pull through. They were already talking about performing open-heart surgery. The doctor told me that only I was allowed in to see my husband, but I insisted on Mrs. Sands going into the room. After all, she had been a critical care nurse and was my supervisor at the hospital. I was fully aware of what patients in Wells's condition looked like, and I needed moral support.

But I wasn't prepared for what I saw as we walked into the room. My tall, vibrant husband's dark skin had taken on an ashen color. *He's a dead man being kept alive by machines, life-support machines beeping and pinging, tubes in his chest and mouth.* I was afraid to get closer, but I had to walk to my husband's side and inspect him. He was helpless, and he needed me.

Mrs. Sands stood by the door as I rubbed Wells's hand. I forced myself to look at him. A nurse came in to check on him, but I barely saw her through my tears. What was going to happen to him? To me? What about the kids?

"Lilly, I'm going to make the phone calls, and I'll be back."

I nodded, and then I pulled the chair up to Wells's bed. I took in the scene, trying to memorize everything. The room was dimly lit, and all I could hear was the machines. I alternated rubbing Wells's hand and kissing it.

"Get better, Wells. Please get better. These machines are helping you. Please get better. We need you. Please."

Mrs. Sands came back and told me that Wells's parents would be up to the hospital within the hour. My mother would stay with the kids. And she couldn't reach Peggy.

When Wells's mother, Minnie McClendon, appeared in the hospital room, I collapsed into her arms. I collected myself enough to step out so his somber father, Herbert "Pops" McClendon, could go into the room.

Minnie was so overcome with emotion that she let go of me and left the room. I followed her. We stood in the hallway near the nurse's station, holding each other and crying.

A nurse came over to us and said she needed to escort us to the consultation room to speak with the doctor. Wells's parents and I sat beside each other. The doctor sat at the head of the long table and said they would have to perform open-heart surgery on my husband within the next couple of days. It was his only chance to survive.

Minnie and I gasped in unison, too stunned to speak. Tears streaked down Pops's round brown face. He massaged his bald head as if he had the worst headache in the world. Minnie's ample chest was heaving up and down, her lips moving as if she wanted to talk, but had no words. And I was staring at the doctor but could barely see him through my tears.

I, along with family and friends, took turns keeping vigil by Wells's side. He was heavily sedated, but when I asked him to squeeze my hand, I could feel some pressure.

--- ◆◆◆ ---

Before his accident, Wells had insisted that I needed to learn to drive. My response had been that I worked five minutes from the apartment, the kids' school was ten minutes away, and downtown was also five minutes away. There were also buses, taxis, and Wells himself for transportation. None of my female relatives had a driver's license. Since I so closely identified with them, it never occurred to me to learn to drive.

"You never know when you'll need to drive. Besides, why wouldn't you want to drive this beautiful new baby?" The "baby" that he had been referring to was his 1966 Dodge Charger.

"Okay," I'd said.

I had gotten my permit, and Wells had started teaching me to drive. Then his accident happened. After the accident, I was dejected and afraid to drive. His car had sat in the parking lot outside of our apartment building since his accident, and I could barely look at it while he was laid up in the hospital.

But after I came home from the hospital one afternoon, I forced myself to look at the deep blue car. It was sleek. I pulled Wells's key from my purse, slowly pulled open the door, and sat down in the driver's side bucket seat. The car still smelled new. I inhaled deeply. With my exhale, I gripped the steering wheel.

What was I going to do about that car? It was like the car was haunting me, taunting me. I was holding out hope that Wells was going to get better and be able to drive his car again. But it was hardly my most pressing issue.

The doctors performed open-heart surgery on Wells and constantly reminded us that they were doing their best for him as he spent several weeks in intensive care.

Finally, he was well enough to be transferred from ICU and then the doctors decided that he could get the best care in the next stage of his recovery at the hospital where I worked. I didn't assist in his care. But each day, I spent my lunch hour with him, as well as some time before and after work. I did all this while eight months pregnant.

Wells was grateful to have me with him. Sometimes we would just sit quietly and hold hands, and I had never felt closer to him. The girls were allowed to visit him as well. He had congestive heart failure, but eventually he was well enough to be released from the hospital. The girls were happy to have him home.

I delivered the baby, Anthony, but nothing was ever the same.

Time passed, and Wells wanted to finish up his degree and return to a normal life. But constant pain and difficulty breathing prevented him. We started arguing on a regular basis, especially about his having alcohol delivered to the apartment and getting drunk.

"Wells, you shouldn't be drinking so much alcohol with your heart problem." I said this to him one day as we were all sitting down to dinner.

"Don't tell me what to do, woman," he snapped.

Anthony was sitting in his high chair making a mess of his food. The girls, by then used to the fighting, continued eating. I no longer had an appetite.

My world was in tatters like the pieces of fabric I cut with the scissors. I was the queen of getting involved with the wrong men. They always started out one way but ended up being mean as the devil. Wells was supposed to have been different. Getting married was supposed to have made the difference.

"I'm not trying to tell you what to do, Wells. I just know that smoking and drinking aren't good for you with your medical problems."

"You let me worry about that."

"Okay, fine. You worry about it then." I was tired of arguing—tired of worrying about a sick husband, three kids, a job, and bills.

"I'm going to deal with you later," Wells said.

I looked at my husband. His words sounded like a threat. None of this was supposed to be happening. It was like my grandparents. Mother used to cower when Grandpa barked at her. I didn't want to be afraid of my husband. I understood that he was sick, frustrated, and unable to work.

I took the baby into the bathroom to wash him up and think in peace. I decided to be extra kind to Wells and more attentive. Maybe that would cause him to behave more lovingly toward me.

My plan didn't work. The sicker he became, the meaner he became. He helped with the kids, but he behaved as though he despised me. I started dreading coming home from work every day.

On one such afternoon, I stopped off at Mama's apartment before going home from work. Mama; Vivian; and her little boy, Warren, lived in the building next to ours. Mama was still doing day work and helping me out with the kids.

Vivian had also gone against Auntie Eula Mae's advice about not having children before marriage. She had two sons by two different men. The boys were about a year apart.

Aunt Bessie and Uncle Slim never had children of their own, so they asked Vivian if they could take care of her youngest boy, Christopher. Vivian turned her son over to them and was fine with their intention to adopt her son.

I knew that I had enough business of my own to mind, but I was confused. "Vivian, why are you giving Christopher away?"

"Because I can't support him. Uncle Slim has a good job, and they can give him more than I can."

"Well, what about Christopher's daddy? Won't he help you with him?"

"I don't want to be bothered with that fool anymore, and Uncle Slim and Aunt Bessie can take better care of Christopher than I can. Besides, they always wanted a child."

But does it have to be your child? I wanted to ask, but I knew any further discussion on the matter would be pointless. I was talking to my baby sister, but I felt like I was talking to a stranger.

Vivian had changed from the spirited person who had desires for a better life. She had turned into someone who was barely able to make it from one day to the next. I dearly loved Vivian, and while my life wasn't a bed of roses, I wanted better for her.

Things quickly went from bad to worse with Vivian as she made the rash decision to marry a man whom she met one night at a nightclub. She was drinking regularly, and she started having more babies.

To make everything worse, Honey suddenly showed up in Buffalo *without her family*! She and her family had moved from Atlanta to Chicago, and Chicago was where she had left them.

Honey went straight from the bus station to stay in Mama's crowded apartment. Already on edge about my personal circumstances, I felt as I observed my sisters' situations that I was about to go over the edge.

Honey came over to say hello to us. I asked her why she had left the kids and Mr. Green.

"I just want to do something different." She was playing with the beads on her pearl necklace. The once long, black hair that bounced when she walked was gone. Her hair was now cut short, in no particular style, and peppered with gray; her eyes told a story of misery.

I admit I had been jealous of Honey when we were younger. Her hair was beautiful, her skin flawless, and she was a free spirit. She never cared what anybody thought about her. But looking at her as she sat in my apartment, I saw she didn't have anything left worth coveting. I would rather have had the old Honey back.

"I'm okay. I told you. I'm just doin' something different."

That *something different* included, just like Vivian, becoming an alcoholic.

Discouragement had doubled down on me and threatened to never let me go. And I was disgusted. How could Honey, or any other woman walk away from her children? Oh, I *could* understand leaving a man, but not your children!

Honey stayed with Mama for a while, but she eventually moved to the West Coast with a boyfriend, who I was told was a drug addict. She moved away with no attempt at being reunited with her children. We rarely heard from Honey after she'd moved.

What was happening to my mother's children, myself included? Wells was sick and verbally abusive. I figured that he didn't know how to handle his new reality, and I certainly didn't know how to deal with him. Our once peaceful, loving relationship had turned into a war.

We even argued about my sewing. Wells told me that I didn't cook and I didn't clean. The only thing I was interested in was sewing. It was a lie because I was contributing a great deal to the household. But I felt truly alive when I was sewing, creating.

When I sewed, I felt as if I was doing something important and special. I would use newspaper and cut out my own pattern designs. I enjoyed making a garment. I felt such a sense of pride and satisfaction as I was putting the finishing touches on the garment. People would ask me where I had gotten something. When I told them I'd made it, they would oftentimes ask me to make them something. My time was limited, but I would lose sleep to work on the item.

Wells offered no support. He only gave me trouble. When I tried to talk to him about my desire to perhaps open a store selling my items, he would tell me that I needed to stick to my job at the hospital and forget about that foolishness.

But I couldn't forget about it. I felt like it was what gave me significance.

I didn't care what he said. Somehow or another, I was going to turn my cherished hobby into something more. One night as I was at the sewing machine, with *The Tonight Show* on, I told myself that God had allowed me to find those magazines in the woods all those years ago because he wanted me to use the gift that he had given me.

⸺ ❖❖❖ ⸺

It had never occurred to me that the arguments between Wells and I were affecting the kids until, one day, Bridgett, who was around twelve years old at the time, brought it to my attention. She and I were walking home from the grocery store when she said, "Ma, I get scared when you and Daddy argue. Can you *please* stop fighting?"

Caught off guard, I had to hold back tears. I told Bridgett I was sorry for scaring her, and I promised her everything was going to be okay.

But everything wasn't okay. In fact, things only got worse. How unfair it was to the kids, I thought. I had brought this man into their lives. He had earned their trust and had become an actual father to them. Almost as suddenly as all the good things had happened, life had begun to erode.

⸺ ❖❖❖ ⸺

Wells and I had stopped fighting long enough for me to get pregnant again. Eleven months after Anthony was born, I gave birth to Regina. About a week after we brought her home from the hospital, she was sleeping in her cradle in our bedroom when Wells and I were fighting again. I don't even remember what the issue was, but Wells was furious. He walked over to the little wooden stowaway table that held my sewing machine. With all his strength, he toppled the table, and my sewing machine went crashing to the floor.

I'd had enough. I fled with all the children in a cab to Wells's parents' house. In the cab, I was sick with despair. Wells and I and the kids had truly been happy. With the accident, everything had fallen apart.

His parents had a nice house on an east side street of well-kept homes. Pops was a jovial man, and I loved him. When he wasn't working, he could be found resting in his brown leather recliner, smoking a pipe, and watching sports or a western.

Minnie fixed dinner for us that evening. Minnie didn't particularly care for me. No one had to tell me that. I hadn't done anything to her, but I knew she didn't like the fact that her son had married a woman with two children by two different men. I knew she thought I was a hussy.

She was polite and tolerated me, but she didn't treat me with any warmth. She was, however, good to the girls, which was the most important thing. Pops, on the other hand, loved *me* as well as the girls.

We all sat down and ate at their large table in the dining room. After dinner, the kids busied themselves with some toys while I talked to my husband's parents. Up to that point, I hadn't disclosed any of our private struggles to them, but now I had to tell them what was going on.

"Lilly, you know Wells is sick. And he's frustrated. He can't work anymore, and he doesn't feel like a real man anymore. But you know he loves you and *all* your kids. He took you and your kids in when he married you," Minnie said.

"Took me in?" I said with a laugh. "I don't mean any disrespect, Minnie, but I didn't need your son to take me in. I had a job *and* a place to live when I met him. Now I believe he's going to kill me." I was surprised how matter-of-factly I had told Wells's mother that I thought her son was going to kill me. I meant exactly what I'd said.

"That's crazy talk," she said. "Wells barely has strength to take care of himself, much less hurt somebody."

Pops was listening to this exchange. The smoke rings from his pipe twirled up toward the ceiling. I hated tobacco smoke, but I enjoyed the aroma that came from a pipe.

"You just need to fix him a nice dinner and talk nice to him," Minnie continued.

"What?" I said with an incredulous laugh. "You don't understand. Have you ever been in this situation?"

"No."

"Then you just don't understand what it's like. I'm doing the best I can. I'm doing everything I know to do. I do love him, and I'm taking care of him and these kids. I just don't understand why he's abusive like this. You shouldn't try to excuse his behavior because he's sick and can't work."

Pops broke his silence. He had a voice so deep that Jewel said it sounded like a frog when he spoke. "I'll have a talk with him tomorrow. Don't you worry, Lilly. Things will work out fine."

"I would appreciate you talking to him. I hope it will do some good. I don't know what I did to make him act like this."

The kids and I spent the night at my in-laws' house. As I lay in the guest room, unable to sleep, I tried to objectively assess the situation. People often lashed out at the person closest to them. That's what Wells was doing to me. Not just his chest, but along with it all his dreams and ambitions, had been crushed in that accident, rendering him hopeless.

The longer I lay in the darkness thinking, the gloomier the situation appeared. All my belated fantasies for a happily ever after had been mangled in that car crash as well.

*** ◆◆◆ ***

It was too late for Pops to talk to Wells. When we got home the next morning, I had to call an ambulance because Wells was having severe chest pains. After several days in the hospital, he had a massive heart attack and died. He passed away before I could make it back to the hospital after taking a break to freshen up and check on the kids.

Celeste and Mike brought me to the hospital. We walked down the hall to Wells's room arm in arm. Wells's brother, sister-in-law, and parents were gathered around his bed when I walked in on jelly legs. The tubes were disconnected, and he lay still on the bed—young and dead. I walked forward to the bed and the family made room for me.

"Wells," I screamed. "Wake up. Please wake up." I fell into Pops's body, sobbing and moaning.

"It's okay, Lilly. Everything's gonna be okay," Pops's deep voice rumbled.

"No, it won't." I didn't believe anything would ever be okay again.

I remember my friends taking me home. I crawled into bed and fell into an uneasy sleep. I dreamed about Wells. He was standing tall and proud in a new suit worn underneath the gown he wore into the auditorium for his college graduation. I woke up before he made it to the stage to receive his diploma.

Auntie LaRue gently shook me. "Lilly. It's time to wake up."

Mama and Auntie were standing over me. I looked out the window. I realized I had been dreaming and Wells wouldn't be receiving his diploma after all his hard work.

I groaned and turned my face to the wall. I wasn't getting up. There was no point.

"Lilly, it's three o'clock in the afternoon. It's time to get up. The baby needs to be fed, and the kids want to see you."

The life had gone out of me, and I had no feeling. I didn't care about anything. Nothing mattered, not even the children. "I'm not gettin' up," I said in a flat voice. The kids didn't have a father anymore, and now they didn't have a mother.

"Lil, you been in the bed since yesterday afternoon. You got to get up now."

"No. Take the kids and go." I turned back to my mother and aunt. I wanted them to see my face. I wanted them to know that I didn't care what happened anymore. They needed to take the kids and leave.

"Okay," Auntie said. "We'll take care of them, but we'll be back tomorrow. You gotta get up, girl. You can't stay in this room for the rest of your life."

I waited for about forty-five minutes, long enough for them to get the kids' stuff together and leave. After I was sure they were gone, I rolled out of the bed and made my way to the bathroom. In the medicine cabinet was the bottle of antianxiety meds that the psychiatrist at the clinic had prescribed for me. I didn't like taking medicine, and I hadn't taken any of the pills. They were to be taken at bedtime due to them causing drowsiness.

I took the pills from the cabinet, filled a cup with a glass of water, locked the bathroom door, and sat down on the floor by the toilet. My heart started pounding. I could feel all the blood rushing to my head as I turned the cap on the bottle. I would have to take them one at a time, as I was afraid to take them at all.

You have to do this, Lilly. You're useless to these kids now. I opened the pill bottle and removed one. I looked at the white pill, holding it between my pinky and thumb. I sat the pill on my tongue and chased it down with the water. The buzz I felt was the same as my first time drinking too much wine. I turned the bottle for another pill, and they all went spilling onto the floor. My fingers felt like I had on winter gloves as I tried to pick them up.

There was a pounding on the bathroom door. "Lil, open the door. Open the door!" It was Celeste.

"No," I said and continued gathering the pills. I put two more in my mouth and chased them down with the rest of the water.

The next thing I remember is waking up the next morning, in my bed, with Celeste sitting on the side of the bed, staring at me with an angry look on her face.

"I knew how many of those pills you took by the count on the bottle. You took three, right?"

She sighed and handed me a warm washcloth, which I used to wipe my face. I was groggy, and my head felt like it was going to explode.

"I told you I was fifteen when my mother died. What I didn't tell you was that I had to be hospitalized and force-fed because I had stopped eating. I felt like, if my mother was dead, there was no point in living anymore. I was the smartest girl in the whole tenth grade class, and my daddy loved me. But if my mother was dead, nothing else mattered."

Celeste paused and slowly nodded her head. "When I tell you I didn't want to live, I mean I was so low and depressed that nothing mattered. But as difficult as life can be sometimes, I'm glad I lived. And you have a lot to live for. Your kids need you, Lil."

"Where are the kids?"

"Well, Bridgett and Jewel are with your mother. Anthony is with your in-laws, and the baby is with your aunt LaRue. They would probably be separated like that if you weren't around."

I was wringing the washcloth tightly and letting tears flow freely down my face. "I didn't really want to die, Celeste. I just don't know how I'm going to make it with four young kids. And I hate them not having a father. It's so unfair. We only had five years. Now I have two more children, and none of them have a father. What am I gonna do?"

"Do the best you can, Lilly. It's not like you're all alone. You have help. Just do the best you can." Celeste hugged me. "We'll help you. You have lots of people who love you. We'll help you."

The morning of the funeral, after awakening from a few restless hours of sleep, my head was still pounding. I looked around the room that Wells and I had shared for five years. I had made all the curtains for my apartment. I had enjoyed taking care of the apartment, making a home for us. Even after Wells's accident and after our relationship had turned sour, I'd still cleaned and polished and sat flowers in the windowsills.

But on this morning, the apartment felt like what it was—a cold contraption made of steel and concrete. I went to the kitchen, ate a slice of bread with peanut butter, and washed some aspirin down with milk.

Then I had all the kids get up so we could hurry up and get dressed and get out of the apartment before I totally lost my composure. I'd bought all the kids new clothes for the funeral. Pops had taken me to the men's shop, where we'd bought a suit, underwear, socks, and shoes for Wells. I wanted him to be put away with dignity.

What made me realize the finality of it all was when Wells's parents and I had met with the funeral director and picked out the casket—a beautiful, shiny black coffin long enough for his six-foot-two frame.

Pops picked Mama, me, and the kids up at the apartment, and we all rode from his house in a funeral home limousine to the church. We didn't belong to a church, so Bill, whom Auntie LaRue had since married, preached the funeral at this church.

Once we were in the church, my kids and Wells's parents sat on the front pew. Mama and the other family members sat in the rows behind them. I took my position, standing by the casket, greeting the mourners. I heard, "He looks so good." "I'm so sorry for your loss." I politely accepted the condolences, but what I wanted to scream was, *What do you mean he looks good? He's dead!*

When the organist started grinding out "Amazing Grace," my knees went weak because the dreaded service was about to begin. Pops appeared by my side and guided me to my seat. When the soloist started singing "Amazing Grace," Minnie let out a loud, guttural cry. Wells's brother put his arms around her, while Pops kept his arm around my shoulder. When one of the church members started reading the obituary and mentioned my name as his wife, I doubled over in agony.

I looked at my kids. All of them were crying. I was sure the little ones didn't fully understand what was going on and only cried because everyone else was crying. My heart especially ached for Bridgett, as she had thoroughly embraced Wells as her dad.

Fate had been so cruel. I hadn't been Wells's wife long enough. Just when we were happy, the rug had been pulled out from all of us.

Throughout his illness, I had never expected him to die. Honestly, a part of me felt a guilty relief that he had died. I honestly feared that he was going to kill me. Maybe it was irrational, being afraid of a sick man.

The service concluded. As we rode in the limousine with my in-laws, I looked at my kids. They were all solemn. I still wasn't the most demonstrative mother, but as we rode back to my in-laws' house, I told them all that their daddy would be proud of them and that I loved them very much.

Sitting by the casket at the graveside, I was determined to keep my composure. I kept myself in a tight, prone posture. Every muscle in my body was taut. *Hold on. Don't let go. Hold on.* When Wells was lowered into the ground, a part of me went into the ground with him. Through no fault of his own, Wells was the third man in a row who had left me—left me with children who had no father.

⸺ ◆◆◆ ⸺

The repast was at Wells's parents' home. As Vivian and I were in the kitchen doing the dishes after the meal, I was relieved that some of the heaviness had lifted from me.

Vivian whispered, "Wells was too mean to live. At least he left you with insurance money. What are you gonna do with it?"

"I loved Wells, Viv. He wasn't always evil. Anyway, I'm not thinking about no insurance money right now." Her insensitivity angered me.

"I'm sorry. I just know what a hard time he gave you after his accident."

We finished the dishes in silence, which gave me a chance to cool off and think. I decided that there was no point in being angry with Vivian. As she dried the dishes, I took a long look at her. I hadn't seen too much of her lately, as she had her hands full fighting with her own no-good man and raising her son, Warren, and four girls she'd given birth to back-to-back.

My sister looked sad and tired. She had dark circles under her eyes. The last time I had been to her house, she was playing a song about somebody jumping off a bridge. She played that song over and over again. It was enough to make anyone depressed and want to find a bridge to jump off.

"You gonna be okay with the kids?" she asked, bringing me back to the present.

"I'll be fine. I wish things had turned out better. It's strange ... Things were good with me and Wells for a pretty good while, and now he's gone." I wiped the tears from my cheeks.

We sat down and were silent for a minute. I was the first to break the silence. "Viv, you know, you helped me so much in the past, and you're still my little sister. What can I do for you?"

"Nothin'. I don't need nothin'."

I wanted to light into Vivian. I wanted to be able to shame her into straightening up. I wanted her to stop drinking, clean up her house, and take better care of her children.

Vivian didn't work outside her home. Her husband had a good paying job at the steel plant. All she had to do was take care of her children and her house. But she couldn't focus on her responsibilities because she was too busy drinking and fighting with her husband.

I only drank water or pop during our partying days, but Vivian always drank alcohol. Acquiring the taste for alcohol was one of the worst things she could have done.

I looked at Vivian and took a deep breath. "I know what," I said cheerfully. "We're gonna get away, even if it's just for a day. Just you and me."

"I can't," Vivian said, with *no* interest in what I had just said.

Minnie pushed the kitchen door open with her wide hip. She sat an empty platter on the table.

"All the guests are gone. Only people still here are family," Minnie said. She burst into tears. "I never thought I would have to bury a child of mine. It's supposed to be the other way around." She covered her face with her large shaking hands and sobbed.

I reached out to touch her wrist, but she pulled away.

"I'm fine. I'm fine." She wiped her face on the blue apron that hugged her ample waist. "There's other things to clear up." She hastily left the kitchen.

I considered Vivian again. Being around her caused the dark cloud to descend on me again, but I promised myself that I was going to do something nice for her when I got the chance.

CHAPTER 10

⋙ ❖❖❖ ⋘

THE TIMING OF Wells's death coincided with the deterioration of living conditions in the projects. Adjusting to being a thirty-one-year-old widow was a lot on its own. Added to that, the projects were becoming an annoying and increasingly dangerous place to live. The two elevators in our apartment building seemed to malfunction more often than not.

"Girl, I'm so tired of these elevators breakin' down," Peggy said one day after we had taken our kids to the grocery store. Both elevators had been working when we'd left for the store. When we came back, the doors to both elevators wouldn't open. Even when the elevators *were* working, they usually reeked of urine.

"I know. I'm tired," I said. "After working all day, I sure don't feel like walkin' up eight flights of stairs."

But complaining wasn't going to get the groceries upstairs, so up we went.

"I told you the kids, Mama, and me got stuck between floors on that thing last week," I said, huffing and puffing my way up the concrete stairs. "Seems like I was pressing that alarm bell for an hour before help came."

When we finally made it to the eighth floor, we were greeted by a man slumped over on the top step. I didn't know if he was dead or alive.

Peggy kicked his leg. He *was* alive. "Move out of the way."

There seemed to always be a junkie sprawled out on the stairs.

"They really need to do somethin' about these damn junkies. And they *need* to do somethin' about anybody and everybody having access to this roof," Peggy said. "The roof door should be locked, and only the super should have the key. What business does anybody have goin' on the roof?"

--- ◆◆◆ ---

"We need to form a tenants' council," Peggy announced one Saturday morning.

We were sitting at Charlotte Hill's kitchen table, drinking coffee. Charlotte was our friend from the fifth floor. She lived with her husband and four teenage children.

Charlotte didn't work. To our knowledge, she wasn't sick. But she walked around in her apartment all day wearing only a nightgown. Sometimes the gowns were see-through, which I thought was simply inappropriate.

"Bennie needs to tell Charlotte to put some clothes on," I whispered to Peggy when Charlotte had gone in the kitchen to get our coffee.

"I know," she said, snickering and shaking her head.

But we didn't have too much to say about Charlotte because her children were staying out of trouble and doing well in school. Her oldest daughter was a freshman in college. The next girl was a senior in high school and had plans to become a pediatrician. Obviously she and her husband were doing something right!

"What's a tenants' council?" Charlotte asked.

"It's when the tenants form a group to address issues in the buildings. For example, we pay our rent every month, so why should we have to deal with broken-down elevators every week? And something really needs to be done about these junkies always passed out on the stairs. I just want to take my foot and shove them so hard they go tumbling down those stairs and break their necks or bust their heads wide open."

"Peggy!" Charlotte said.

"What? That's how I feel."

"I know what you mean," I chimed in.

"So who do we talk to about all these bad things going on around here?" Charlotte asked.

"We can start with the super," Peggy said. "Ollie thinks I'm ridiculous for even wantin' to do something like this. But shoot, we pay rent here.

They need to maintain these buildings better than they do. It wasn't like this when we first moved in here."

"I know. Everything was beautiful then, but nobody cares anymore. And you know, a few Negroes have to ruin it for everybody. Bennie and me are thinking about moving outta here," Charlotte said.

"Where you gonna move to?" I asked. At that moment, a seed was planted: *I'm moving,* I told myself.

"We're not sure yet. We just started talkin' about it. Anyway, maybe this tenant council will help with some of this mess going on around here. Have y'all talked to anybody else about this?"

"Not yet, but we will," Peggy said. "Something's got to change. The worst problem of all is these gangs. It's ridiculous. They're trying to take over the projects. The other day I was coming home. I happened to look up, and I saw two of them standin' on the roof of our building. They were pointin' a shotgun as if they were gonna shoot me. I ran into the building, but I was afraid to ride up to our floor."

Peggy always seemed to be fearless, but I could see the crack in her armor. The projects were getting to her.

Charlotte agreed to help us in our attempt to form a tenants' council. The three of us went to the manager's office. He was a small black man who had no time for foolishness, and he let us know it.

"If you all can get six other adults in the projects interested in your idea, come back to me with the names, and we will take it from there."

We thought the most efficient way to go about it was to have one of Charlotte's daughters type up a flyer and put it on the bulletin board of all eight buildings. If anyone was interested, we asked them to write his or her name and number on the paper, and we would contact them. We also talked to neighbors as we were out and about.

Most of the residents had never heard of a tenants' council and were skeptical about it making any difference. Many of the residents were planning on moving, so they didn't care about things getting any better.

I had to be honest with myself. I was trying to hang onto the past, when life had been good in the projects. But everything was going down. Management could barely maintain the buildings, and they seemed ill equipped to handle the gang problem.

The idea of a tenants' council was too little too late, and I soon lost interest. With a job and kids to raise, it wasn't worth the effort. I needed to *move*. Period.

We had once enjoyed living in the projects, but no more. Lewdness, lawlessness, and fear began to permeate the halls of our buildings. If the walls could talk …

One night, I heard a woman down the hall from me crying out for help. Over and over again, she cried, "Peggy, help me." In the morning, that woman was found dead.

The memory still haunts me. Why didn't I help? Why didn't anyone else help her? That incident instilled a fear in me that I walked around with every moment of the rest of my time residing in the Tennyson Mall.

"Life sure was better before they started allowing all these gangsters and thugs in here," Peggy said. "Now we have people getting murdered right here in the building. This is real scary."

"I'm telling you," I said in agreement.

The woman who was murdered was Peggy's brother's girlfriend. Her brother also lived on our floor; a gang member was later arrested for her rape and murder.

The gangs who were wreaking havoc where we lived were the Cobras and the East Side Lovers. Initially only married couples and their children could move into the complex. At some point, the policy was changed, allowing anyone to move in. With the policy change, conditions declined so badly that eventually mayhem reigned.

The gang members marked their territory with graffiti on the inside walls of the buildings and the exterior red brick.

Things were so bad Jewel was afraid to take the garbage out to the incinerator, which was right outside our apartment door. I knew she was afraid because of the violence. In hindsight, I realized that simply opening the incinerator door and looking into the roaring fire was enough to scare any young kid.

⚫ ◆◆◆ ⚫

I could only see his eyes. Everything else was hidden, covered in black. Black jacket. Black pants. Black leather gloves. The black scarf covered all but his dark, beady eyes.

He cornered me on the roof of my building. I was trapped because he stood in front of the closed steel door. My heart was thumping and my eyes were wide from sheer terror. I looked around, my head sweeping to the left and then to the right. I was nauseous, thinking my only escape from this madman would be to jump eight floors to my certain death. I would smash to the ground, and my children would be orphans.

Please, mister, I mouthed, inaudibly. Then in a shrill voice, I said, "Please let me go home to my kids."

Desperately I lunged for the doorknob, and the man shoved me so violently I fell to the ground. But I hopped back up. This time, I ran at him and gave him a hard kick in the crotch. While he doubled over in pain, I got away.

But I didn't run to my apartment. Instead, I ran for my life. I flew down the stairs, skipping multiple stairs at a time. When I reached the first-floor stairwell, I yanked the door open. I ran through the vestibule, past the wall of tenant mailboxes, and out the door into the light of day. Once I had made it to the common area, where people were coming and going, I knew I was safe.

I awoke from my recurring nightmare in the middle of the night. As I normally did, I got up and went to check to make sure the steel door of my apartment was locked and the chain was still in place. I had come to loathe nightfall.

Sometimes when I couldn't make sense of the evil things people did, this Bible verse came to mind—the heart of man is desperately wicked above all else, who can know it. The complex had once been a desirable place to live, but that all changed as the population changed.

People would set fires and then call the fire department. When they'd respond, the firemen had to be escorted by the police due to threats on their lives.

The mail carriers would come to deliver the mail. If they didn't have someone's welfare check, they would get jumped. Eventually the police had to escort the mail carriers as well.

The one bright spot in life seemed to be that the kids enjoyed school and did well. I had scraped the money together to put the children in Catholic school. I felt that they could get a better education there as opposed to public school.

They did complain about one of the teachers, Sister Innocent. She would hit the students on the palm of the hand with a ruler as punishment for some minor offense.

"She not Sister Innocent. She Sister Guilty," little Anthony would say.

Jewel came home with news one afternoon. "Mom, I have a new friend. Her name is Sandy Sepulveda and she's from Puerto Rico. She's beautiful, and she said she can teach me some Spanish."

--- ❖❖❖ ---

Charlotte and her daughter Debbie appeared at my door one evening. As soon as I opened the door, Charlotte whispered to me, "Girl, do you know who just moved in next door to you?"

"No," I replied.

We stepped into the living room where my kids were entertaining their friends. They had popped popcorn and were dancing to the Jackson 5.

Charlotte had the uncanny ability to know about the goings-on in all eight buildings in the complex. She would serve up information on people, and sometimes I would just laugh. Half the time I didn't know what was true or even who she was talking about.

But this particular day, I wasn't in the mood for any of her gossip. And I was nervous because she seemed to be delivering bad news.

Charlotte, Debbie, and I huddled together.

"Are you talkin' about that mother and her kids right next door to me?" I asked.

"Yes, girl. The oldest son is twenty-three years old, and he's the vice president of the Cobras."

My heart sank and I shuddered with fear.

Charlotte was still whispering. "And the mother has the nerve to be a missionary in God's Church of Christ, over on Michigan Avenue. The guy's name is Leon Stevens. And those nappy-headed brothers of his and the sister, they're all disciples."

Debbie remained silent. She had probably come with Charlotte to be her bodyguard. Few people traveled around the complex alone anymore.

I envied the second part of Charlotte's news. She said, "Me and Bennie finally bought a house. Praise the Lord, as soon as it closes, we're gettin' outta dodge. Listen, girl—I just wanted to come and tell you so you could be more careful. Watch your kids. I gotta go."

Was that why I had that nightmare? Was it an omen?

Upon opening my apartment door, my view was the wall. There were two apartments to my right, both of them no more than a couple of feet away. The new family had the corner apartment—too close for comfort.

Because of my time spent living in the projects, I've never wanted to live in another apartment building. I don't know if it is ever a good idea to have so many different people practically stacked on top of each other like that.

The motley crew Charlotte was talking about consisted of two unkempt teenage boys, a little boy, a teenage girl, a young man, and a dowdily dressed mother. The males always looked like they left home without washing up, changing clothes, or combing their hair. The girl's hair was always perfectly coiffed, but they all looked angry and menacing.

After Charlotte left, I told the kids' friends to go home, and I told my kids to get ready for bed. It was still early, and the kids protested. But I needed to be alone with my six-pack of beer and figure out what I was going to do.

I had picked up the beer-drinking habit from attending Peggy and her husband's house parties. Years before, Rosalie had been so angry with Grandpa because he was always cussing, but he forbade her to cuss. She called him a hypocrite. I felt like a hypocrite for being so down on Wells and Vivian for drinking alcohol, and here I was doing the same thing. But then, in a way, I could understand them drinking; it took the edge off the sharp corners of life.

For some reason, I was in possession of the family Bible, which sat on my coffee table, rarely touched. It was at least six inches thick and filled with pictures of biblical scenes. A picture of a blond, blue-eyed Jesus graced the frayed-at-the-edges cover. The first few pages contained our incomplete family tree.

I picked up the Bible, and while drinking my beer, I tried to find something that I could easily understand. I skipped through page after page until I came to Psalm 23.

My eyes were bleary from a combination of fatigue and beer, but I read:
The Lord is my shepherd.

I slammed the Bible closed. The words had no impact. I dropped the Bible back down on the coffee table and headed for bed. First, though, I stumbled to the door to check the lock. I made sure the chain was secure. I kept the kitchen and the living room lights on and made my way down the hall to my bedroom.

I fell on the bed. It was spinning—like my life, spinning out of control. My sleep was always disturbed by nightmares and the scream of emergency vehicles.

Soon after moving in, the gang leader was stabbed to death in the field across from our building. Even young kids were getting killed in the projects. I was worried sick that one of my kids would be next or that I would be raped and murdered. When I talked to Peggy or Mama about my fears, I would temporarily feel better. But when I was in bed at night, a book or television show couldn't keep me distracted from what I feared the most.

--- ◆◆◆ ---

I was also concerned about my mother, but she wasn't as nervous as I was. I encouraged her to hurry up and find other living arrangements. I reminded her that, since she was alone, it would be easier for her to find a place and move.

Paradise was now hell. I needed to move, but I wasn't really sure where to go. I was glad I had not spent any of the life insurance money Wells had left me. I would use that for the move. I was also getting survivor's benefits, so money wasn't a major issue. *Where to move* was the major issue.

Auntie LaRue had married the Baptist preacher who owned the diner where I'd worked as a teen. My aunt and her husband had purchased a large, two-family home in Hamlin Park. Thankfully, they rescued Mama from the projects by renting her the upstairs apartment; it was roomy, bright, airy, and the nicest place that my mother had ever lived in.

When she lived in the projects, Mama never opened her dark, heavy curtains. She didn't want anyone looking in and seeing what she was doing. For her new apartment, she bought lacy white curtains, and she put houseplants on every windowsill in every room.

Mama's kitchen had lots of counter space, giving her room to work her culinary magic. She would make "cha cha," which consisted of various combinations of fresh vegetables, spices, and vinegar. We would put the cha cha over collard or mustard greens. It had a somewhat sweet, tangy taste, and it was delicious. Another family favorite was Mama's melt-in-your mouth chicken with dumplings.

Mama came alive like I had never seen her before. It had always been in the back of my mind that she would have another breakdown. After her move, I never worried about that again. *And* she met a nice gentleman friend to keep company with.

Auntie LaRue, like Eula Mae, was a strong advocate of education. She actually studied the dictionary as well as her encyclopedia set. She was also a wealth of practical information.

On Memorial Day, the kids and I went to visit Mama and Auntie LaRue. Bill barbequed while the kids played in the large backyard.

The neighborhood kids loved to come to my aunt's house. Her porch—the porch was adorned in white wicker. There were two chairs, a love seat, a table, an array of flowers in pots, and a bookshelf that held some of her beloved books.

Being at my aunt's house gave me a bit of rest from my troubled life. "You should have been a teacher, Auntie LaRue," I said as we drank lemonade.

"I *am* a teacher," she said with a smile. Auntie LaRue had a musical voice, and I loved to listen to her talk.

All of my aunts were intelligent, self-taught women. I believe if my aunts had been born in a different era, one where black people had more educational opportunities and didn't have to begin working at such a young age, they would have had successful careers.

My mother was the only one of the sisters who didn't read or write well. The only thing she ever read was a few passages from the Bible. Mama excelled in what she enjoyed, which was cooking, gardening, and quilting.

My aunts had a big impact on my life by helping me however they could and by modeling womanhood. I admired them, even Aunt Bessie. They had all taken the lemons they'd been dealt in life and made their own version of lemonade.

Mama had been my rock. She was my biggest defender and biggest cheerleader. She never accomplished anything that would go down in history, but she did the best she could with what she had, and her love was unwavering.

As the three of us sat on the porch, I told my aunt how afraid I was living in the projects and that I needed to move. She suggested that I get in touch with HUD.

"I don't know anything about HUD," I told her.

"HUD is the Department of Housing and Urban Development. They deal with housing issues, and they should be able to help you." She gave me the number from the phone book.

I called the next day and was given an appointment right away.

••• ◆◆◆ •••

I went downtown to the HUD office after work and poured my heart out to those people. I told them that I was a widow with four young children, and I needed to provide a safer environment for them to grow up in.

I was desperate and ready to beg for help, but there was no need. The HUD office was in the business of assisting people in my situation. My options were to have a new home built or to purchase an existing home.

After the meeting, the words *new home* kept going over and over in my mind. A house built just for me and my children! I could hardly remember anything else that had been discussed.

When I met with the real estate agent, Mr. Tate, I told him that I was living in hell. I remember him as a tall middle-aged man who was soft-spoken and empathetic. He seemed to listen to every single word I said so he would know how to help me.

We went over my options, which were to buy an existing home or to have a home built in the northern suburb of Linwood or in the south town of Malone. We started looking at homes right away. I couldn't afford to live in the expensive parts of Buffalo. After a couple of weeks, I told the agent that I wanted to have a house built.

I was familiar with Linwood but not Malone, so I asked Peggy if she knew anything about Malone. She said the town was beautiful and peaceful and close to the county fair. Mr. Tate drove me to Malone, a scenic ride along the lake. To the left were large expensive homes and a Catholic high school. We passed a library and more homes. Then we turned down Loveland Road, where a small homey-looking hotel sat on the corner. We passed the elementary school, which was surrounded by lots of green space. I was amazed that I had been living in Western New York all those years but had never ventured out that way.

I recalled Mother's pecan farm and the excitement Vivian and I had felt when we'd found out that our grandparents were having a home built in the Bottom. The house had been modest, but it had been brand new. And Grandpa and Mother had no longer been tenant farmers. The house had belonged to them. I would be able to say the same.

The majority of the houses in the city were built very close to one another. Our house was going to be one of only three on about an acre of land. The community was filled with houses but with plenty of space in between each one.

When I met with the builder, he told me he had been expecting a much older woman. At the time of our meeting, I was still thirty-two years old. We went over the plans. The house was going to have four bedrooms, with a half bath on the second floor. Just like most of the others in the area, the house would be white and set on a large back and front yard. Behind the backyard was a large grass-covered field, where Mr. Tate said the neighborhood kids played baseball. The hill behind the house was used for sledding during the winter months.

When I saw the yard, I immediately planned on buying a slide and swing set and having a large aboveground pool installed.

Each house in the neighborhood had a distinct character all its own. Ours would be built between two existing homes. One of the houses was small, with a family of three living in it. The other house was a sprawling ranch with a porch from end to end and a large willow tree in the front.

Across the street, the corner house seemed to be out of place. It was a large, beautiful gingerbread house that I thought fit in better with the expensive homes across the road from the lake.

Mr. Tate said the state park and beach were a short drive away. We also had access to the town beach, which was only for residents. I knew that the kids and I would be going to the beach every chance we got.

At the end of taking care of all the financial business for the house, all I had to pay was fifty-three cents in closing costs. The building of the house got underway in fall 1970. I was excited, but it also gave me one more thing to become anxious about.

CHAPTER 11

❖❖❖

EVER SINCE THE woman was killed in my apartment building, I had been scared out of my wits. I could hardly wait for the house to be built. I'm ashamed to say that incident had much to do with me getting into a relationship with a man named Hollis Bowens. From the day I met Hollis, I didn't like him. Even with a broken leg and broken ribs, he managed to be loud and obnoxious.

He was in the hospital for more than a couple of weeks. I helped him bathe, changed his bed, took his vital signs, and administered his medications. Every day when I did those things, he would ask me when we were going out on a date.

"Mr. Bowens, you're a patient in the hospital," I said as I washed his hairy back. "How are you gonna take anybody out anywhere?"

"Oh, I'm getting outta here soon, ma'am. And I want to take you out on the town."

"I don't think so. But thank you anyway. I'm flattered."

I told Hollis I lived in the projects, but I didn't think he was going to hunt me down. He found out the building and apartment I lived in and began his pursuit in earnest. He would come to my apartment. If I wasn't home, he would slide a record under my door with a handwritten note asking me out for a date. The songs were usually love songs, like Stevie Wonder's, "My Cherie Amour."

I loved that song, but Hollis got on my nerves. I emphatically told him that I didn't like him. "You're arrogant, and you're *loud*." I wasn't normally that bold, and I certainly didn't go around insulting people, but I wanted

Hollis to leave me alone. Even after telling him off, he still persisted. I wondered if he was crazy.

Management sponsored a picnic for the tenants every August. The picnic was like a holiday. Kids got new outfits, ladies got their hair done, and the men barbecued hot dogs and hamburgers on grills large enough to roast a pig.

There was a lot of eating, laughing, and dancing to James Brown music blaring from a radio. Hollis, who often visited an aunt who lived in the building next to mine, came to the final complex picnic.

Against my better judgment, I unenthusiastically said to Hollis, "Okay, I'll have lunch with you in the cafeteria at my job."

"That's romantic," he said.

I bit my tongue because I didn't want to continue to be rude to the man. Even so, I didn't think our lunch would result in a relationship, especially since I had a ready-made family. He knew about my kids but didn't seem to be deterred.

Hollis came to the hospital cafeteria. We had lunch at a small corner table.

"Why are you so interested in me?"

"I like you. You're pretty. It's not just looks though. You a fine lady," he said, smiling.

"Thank you. But I just want you to know that a relationship with a man is not a priority in my life right now. I've had a whole lotta trouble with men, and I'm not looking for any more. And I have way too much going on to get involved with anyone right now."

"You won't get any trouble from this direction."

There *was something* irresistible about Hollis Bowens. Perhaps it had to do with his persistence. He was a mechanic, and yes, he *was* handsome. I was told the reason I had been getting sideways looks from some of the women around the projects was because Hollis was interested in me and not them. They really could have had him if they wanted him. I really didn't care.

"Let's go out on a date," he said, "a real date. This lunch doesn't count."

A snake tattoo stretched the length of his left arm, a memento from his time in the air force. When Hollis told me his father was Irish and his mother was black, I was surprised because he was darker than me. He wore his long, wavy hair in a ponytail. Hollis didn't care for his mother very much because she was a party woman who had neglected him. He said the bravest thing she'd ever done was marry an Irishman when both families had frowned upon it. On the other hand, he idolized his deceased father, who had been the nurturer.

I was crunching my salad and eating a grilled cheese sandwich, but Hollis had hardly touched his food. He was too busy looking at me and smiling.

"Are you crazy?" I asked.

He laughed. I didn't. On the outside I was cool, but on the inside, I was anxious. Anxiety had become my constant companion, and my stomach was often upset.

"Crazy about you," he replied.

I rolled my eyes. "You don't even know me."

"I know enough about you to know that I want you to give me some more of your time."

I thought a minute. He knew that I was a widow with four children. "You're not married, are you?" I asked.

Hollis was divorced and childless. I agreed to go out on a date with him under the condition that we take the kids with us.

"What kind of date is that?" he asked. "First the hospital cafeteria, now the kids."

"It's the only kind I'm goin' on," I said.

We took the kids for a drive to Niagara Falls.

Hollis had been in a couple of bar fights since leaving the air force and had spent a weekend in jail. He had a gun, and he'd said, "I ain't afraid of no gangs. I'll pop a cap in a nigga."

I still wasn't crazy about Hollis, but I needed some semblance of security during the last couple of months of our time in the projects while the house was being built. I lived in fear every day. The kids weren't allowed to play outside anymore, and I tried not to get caught out after dark. I had a switchblade at the ready and prayed while entering the building that I wouldn't have to use it on any miscreants in the elevator or stairwell.

The pace of the building's emptying out picked up significantly. Most days moving trucks were hauling away tenants' belongings. It was sad to see the life being drained from our once thriving complex, the buildings becoming eight nearly empty shells. But I was also happy that my turn was coming very soon.

Hollis started spending more time at my apartment. I gave him my body, but he never had my heart. Once in a while, he would drop a hint about us getting married. I would say something about waiting until we moved, knowing I had no desire to marry him.

--- ❖❖❖ ---

When the house was completed and moving day finally arrived, relief massaged every muscle of my body. No longer would I worry about myself and the kids making it up to our apartment unharmed. No more involuntarily hiking up eight flights of stairs. Gone would be the nightmares and screaming police sirens. The kids, Mama, and I had brought downstairs every box and bag that we could manage and waited in the lobby of the building for Hollis and his friends to pull up in the moving van.

"You all didn't have to bring this stuff down," Hollis said as he met us in the lobby. He had a dolly with him, along with two friends to assist him.

"I know," I said, "but we're just anxious to get goin'."

The elation I felt when I locked the apartment door and gave the key to the super was only superseded by the joy I felt unlocking the door to my brand-new home. The kids were excited and staked claim to their bedrooms, filling the rooms with their belongings.

I look back now on how foolish I had been in so many ways—one of them being the fact that Hollis and I had never discussed him moving in with us. While I was thinking that we would just naturally part ways (I no longer needed him), his plan was to move in with us, which he did. His belongings were on the truck right along the rest of ours!

--- ❖❖❖ ---

A couple of weeks after we moved to Malone, a sledgehammer of news crashed down on me, shattering my excitement about new homeownership.

It was 1971. Jewel had recently turned thirteen years old. We were eating dinner, and she casually told me she had a lump on her neck. I inspected her neck. It was a large lump on the left side, and I wondered how I had missed it. What I had noticed was that she'd gained a lot of weight.

The next day, I told a couple of the nurses at work about the lump. They suggested I take Jewel to the pediatrician as soon as possible.

I immediately made an appointment for Jewel to be seen at the children's hospital. She and I took the bus to the appointment. Jewel busied herself reading a *Right On!* magazine. Jewel didn't seemed to be fazed, but I had something additional to be anxious about. Trying to take my mind off what I didn't know, I crocheted her a vest. After the doctor examined Jewel, with a serious look on his face, he escorted us into his office and invited us to sit down.

"Jewel," Dr. DeSoto said, "how would you like to go down to the cafeteria with one of our volunteers to get a snack?"

"Okay," she answered. "Can I go, Ma?"

"Yes," I said, my stomach doing flip-flops.

Dr. DeSoto, a young man with a Hispanic accent, called for a volunteer to take Jewel down to the cafeteria. When the woman arrived, the doctor gave her a food voucher and told her that we would need about thirty minutes.

"Mrs. McClendon, Jewel has an enlarged lymph node, which needs to be biopsied." He had cleared his throat. "I need to be straightforward with you. Upon examination, I suspect that Jewel has Hodgkin's disease."

He read my puzzled look. I had never heard of that disease before.

"Of course, we won't know for sure until all the testing your daughter needs to have done is complete. But Hodgkin's disease is a rare cancer of the lymphatic system."

Life has a way of serving up these seemingly random, surreal situations, as if to say, *Here you go. Deal with this!* I felt like my body was glued to the chair. My body was locked, and I couldn't move. *What are you talking about, cancer?* My body was frozen, my lips wouldn't open, my eyes trained on the doctor, and my mind was screaming.

How was it that I had escaped the terror of the projects only to be told a few weeks later that my shy, harmless child might have a deadly disease? Why? Was God punishing me? Was this a case of the punishment of the mother being visited on the child?

What?! my mind screamed.

No, the doctor couldn't tell me definitively that Jewel had cancer, but his demeanor told me something serious was going on inside my daughter's body.

After giving me as much information as he could, Dr. DeSoto asked me if there was someone he could call for me.

As time went on, I would find Dr. DeSoto to be a caring man, who kept abreast of the latest treatments for pediatric cancer patients.

I told him that, yes, I would like him to call my Aunt LaRue's house. I took the phone and asked her if she could pick Jewel and me up and take us home. She and her husband came right away.

The night before the biopsy, Jewel asked me why she needed to have the procedure done.

"The doctors just want to find out why you have that lump on your neck." I didn't have the heart to tell the child she might have cancer. And I didn't believe I should until we knew for sure.

⁓ ◆◆◆ ⁓

I nervously awaited Jewel's biopsy results. When I finally got the phone call from the hospital, I was told Jewel needed to come in for one more test, a spinal tap, which would confirm the suspected diagnosis.

Even without the spinal tap, I knew that Jewel had cancer. On the day of the procedure, I had Mama come to the house to be there when the kids came home from school.

After the spinal tap, I met with Dr. DeSoto, without Jewel present. "Mrs. McClendon, all the testing concludes that Jewel does, indeed, have Hodgkin's disease."

I didn't know how to process that information. Even though I had suspected what the outcome of the all the testing would be, hearing the words sent me reeling. I felt hopeless. Suddenly, my new home meant nothing. I wanted to give up on everything.

Was life meant to be just one constant struggle? It seemed like I had been struggling since the day I was born. I was thirty-two, and I was tired.

After my meeting with the doctor, I caught the bus downtown and took a slow walk to Chippewa Street, to the earring store. It was the place I usually made my way to after I would stop off and buy the kids more toys that they didn't need.

I often went to the earring store even if I wasn't planning on buying anything. I just liked to browse. Hundreds of earrings hung on the walls— hoops, pearls, expensive ones, cheap ones, vintage dangling earrings.

I got to know the owners of the earrings shop. They were a sweet diminutive couple. Both had thick Italian accents. The Marconis lived in North Buffalo, and their son and daughter-in-law operated another jewelry store that the couple owned. They were both teenagers when they immigrated to America with their parents. The funny thing was that they were from the same village in Italy but had never met each other until they came to Buffalo.

Mrs. Marconi would always ask me how my children were doing. Whenever I bought two pairs of earrings, she or her husband would always give me a discount on the third pair or slide them into the bag for free.

I remember Mrs. Marconi as though I'd just seen her a minute ago. She was an intense, passionate woman. Her mother was elderly, and her faculties were failing. The elderly woman was prone to wander off, but Mrs. Marconi refused to have anyone else take care of her mother. So she and her husband brought her mother to work every day.

I walked into the store and looked at the walls covered with earrings, but the store didn't hold the same magic. I felt like I had made a mistake and should have just gone straight home to figure out how to tell Jewel that she had cancer.

There were a few customers in the store looking at the walls full of earrings, and Mrs. Marconi was assisting one of them. I turned to walk out when Mrs. Marconi said, "Hello, Mrs. McClendon. How are you today?"

"I'm fine," I lied.

Mrs. Marconi's cheerful greeting made me want to cry, but I couldn't do that in front of their customers.

"What's the matter?" Mrs. Marconi asked as she came over to me.

"Nothing's wrong."

"I think something's wrong. You look like you have trouble."

I had known Mrs. Marconi and her husband for at least five years. Why couldn't I confide in her? I decided that there was no reason why I couldn't.

"My daughter, Jewel, has cancer," I whispered. "She has Hodgkin's disease." I practically choked on my words.

"Oh no. Your beautiful girl with the poofy hair? What you call her hair?"

"An afro."

"Yes. Afro." Mrs. Marconi was stunned. She cupped her jaws with her beefy hands. She pulled me to her, and I bent down so that we could embrace. We disengaged, and she took me by the hand. She told her husband that she would be right back, and we stepped outside.

"What you need from me? What do you need Mr. Marconi and me to do for you?"

"Nothing," I said, smiling and wiping tears away with the back of my hand.

Mrs. Marconi had brought joy to my heart, and she didn't even know it. Her concern for me was a gift.

"Why you smile when you just tell me such terrible news?"

"Because you're a very nice lady, Mrs. Marconi."

She insisted on giving me a ride home. I protested, reminding her that I no longer lived downtown. I told her I didn't want them to go to any trouble for me, but Mrs. Marconi went back into the store and told her husband they had to close the store for a while. She put the Closed sign on the door, and they drove me home.

I was sitting up front with Mr. Marconi so his wife could sit in the back with her mother. As we were riding along Route 5, he kidded with his wife. "It's nice out here, sweetheart. Maybe we buy a house out here," he said with a laugh. His wife just laughed, knowing that her husband was only joking.

When the car pulled into my driveway, Mrs. Marconi said, "If you need something, you let us know, and we be happy to help you. And I pray for Jewel. You tell her I pray for her."

••• ❖❖❖ •••

How do you tell a thirteen-year-old she has cancer? I dreaded it, but I knew that I wasn't going to be able to sleep if I didn't. So after the other kids were in bed, I had her stay in the living room with me and Hollis, and I broke the news to her. She took it in stride. She didn't have much of a reaction to the news. She only asked when the surgery was scheduled and how much it would hurt.

The plan for treatment was a splenectomy at Children's Hospital. Then, after she'd recovered from the surgery, she would have mantle radiation treatment at Caldwell Cancer Institute. The doctors wanted to give Jewel chemotherapy in addition to the radiation, but I refused, believing that would be too stressful on her body.

The splenectomy was a preventative but necessary surgery because the lymphoma could possibly affect the spleen. Mantle field radiation was a type of strong X-ray delivered to the neck, chest, underarms and upper abdomen; it covered all the main lymph node areas in the upper half of the body.

Auntie LaRue suggested that we have a family dinner at my house before Jewel's surgery. Auntie LaRue; Rhonda; and her son, Paulie, flew in from California for our special dinner. They blessed me with money to use for any expenses that might come up regarding Jewel's surgery. Rosalie couldn't make it because she couldn't get the time off from work.

In my kitchen, my mother and her sisters were all together again for the first time in several years. They had a good time reminiscing, and we took a picture of the sisters that showed how much they favored each other, especially Aunt Bessie and Auntie Eula Mae.

Rhonda had married into wealth. Her husband belonged to a Jewish family who owned several upscale men's clothing stores on the West Coast, along with property in California, Florida, and New York.

Rhonda and her husband had homes in Los Angeles, Long Island, and Key West. She had begun to take trips around the world. Among other places, she had been to Paris and London. It was so good to see them, and it was remarkable how different all our lives were from our humble beginnings!

Vivian was also at the gathering, along with her son and four girls. I took a good look at her face and wondered if she had ever found any joy in life. Her shoulders were hunched forward, as if she carried something heavy on her back. I had been so busy with my own life that I hadn't seen very much of my sister in recent months. I felt guilty about not having followed up with making a date for our getaway.

••• ❖❖❖ •••

After the gathering at my house, the next time I saw Vivian, she was in the intensive care unit of the general hospital. She had suffered a massive stroke. Hypertension was a problem in our family. The doctor told us that Vivian's blood pressure reading was ridiculously high. If she had been taking her medications as prescribed, perhaps she would not have had the stroke.

When Mama and I went to see Vivian, she appeared to be on the mend. Although she was paralyzed on one side and still unable to speak, she had regained consciousness and was alert and eating. Her condition had been upgraded to stable, and she actually looked better than she had in a long time. But within the next couple of days, Viv was dead.

Our farewell to Vivian was almost more than I could bear. She had no friends or coworkers, so the church was mostly empty. Her husband, dressed up in a black suit and surrounded by his children, had the nerve to be crying. It took every ounce of self-control for me not to cuss him out.

Vivian's death was a tragedy, and the heavy weight of sadness I felt at my sister's passing was directly related to opportunities I felt were lost—so many of them. I had encouraged her to go ahead and get her driver's license and pursue becoming a city bus driver, but she hadn't. I had told her that she needed to leave her husband, at least separate from him for a while because of their incessant fighting, but she hadn't.

My heart ached for the life that had been lived in so much turmoil. I sobbed uncontrollably and left the church in the middle of her funeral. I wanted to smack her husband on my way out of the building because he was dabbing his eyes with a handkerchief. I didn't think he had a right to be at the funeral, much less sitting there crying.

Mama grieved for Vivian, but she took Vivian's passing better than I thought she would have. Her concern turned to the children. Much to our surprise, with help from his family, Viv's husband wound up taking good care of his daughters and Warren.

CHAPTER 12

❖❖❖

JEWEL HAD CANCER. Vivian passed away. Then I found out that Regina had a potentially fatal blood disorder.

When we moved to Malone, Regina was nine years old. From the time she was a toddler, she had been complaining off and on about arm and leg pain. I would take her to the pediatrician, but he was never able to get to the source of her problem. He would see her every few months and prescribe more medication. I had to take her to the emergency room several times because of the pain, and she would be sent home on pain meds with instructions to see her pediatrician.

Watching Regina suffer was agonizing. I was frustrated and angry because I didn't know what was wrong with her. My anxiety level was shooting through the roof, and I constantly found myself saying that I wanted to run away.

I envisioned myself packing a bag and then taking the long walk down the road to catch the bus downtown to the Greyhound bus station and going someplace where no one could ever find me. I would call Mama and tell her that she would have to come and get the kids. But alas, I couldn't abandon them.

Finally, Wells's mother intervened. She had done some inquiring and was given the name of a doctor who might be able to help us. This time, through blood testing, we were able to find out the source of her problem. I found myself once again sitting in a doctor's office being delivered bad news about a child of mine.

The routine was sadly familiar. The middle-aged pediatrician I took

Regina to was in private practice. He gave her a thorough examination and then instructed her to dress and wait in the waiting room. He stood, his arms crossed, and I sat in a tiny chair looking up at him. His sour countenance was fitting for the news that he gave me after Regina dressed and went back to the waiting room.

"Mrs. McClendon, I'm sorry to inform you that your daughter has sickle cell anemia."

This diagnosis came as we were awaiting Jewel's surgery. And while I hadn't known anything about Hodgkin's lymphoma, I was familiar enough with sickle cell anemia to know it was an inherited blood disorder where the red blood cells were abnormally shaped. Regina's painful episodes were called *crises*.

"Among other possible complications, Regina could suffer a stroke and organ damage," the pediatrician continued. "I have to be frank with you, the survival rate of children with sickle cell is grim; often they die by the time they're fourteen years old."

Tears freely flowed down my cheeks and my neck. I shuddered, and the man handed me some tissues. I hated that man who delivered the bad news. He showed no empathy or compassion. But I believed he knew what he was talking about.

"So what are we supposed to do?"

He wrote a prescription for opioids, and I was instructed to make sure she stayed hydrated. "I want to see her every few months, and don't hesitate to call the office if she has a problem."

Regina was a smart, cheerful little girl who seemed to handle her illness as an inconvenience more than anything else. She adapted well to the new elementary school, and she made fast friends with the two little girls who lived across the street in the gingerbread house.

After getting Regina's diagnosis, I had the other kids' blood tested. They all had sickle cell trait. Much to my relief, I was told the trait doesn't normally cause complications.

Although the other two were sick, I had concerns about Bridgett and Anthony. I felt as though Bridgett wasn't getting enough attention from me. She was doing well in school, and even though she hated housework, she sang while she did it, knowing that she was helping me out. She was a mature girl and also helped out with her siblings. I paid for guitar lessons, and she loved being in the school chorus.

Anthony, bless him, seemed to be totally oblivious to his problem. Anthony and Regina were practically twins, having been born eleven months apart and sharing the same happy-go-lucky personalities. He had also adapted well to his new environment. It was me who was fretting over the fact that he didn't have a dad.

Hollis hardly spent any time with my son. He didn't seem to care too much for Anthony. I wanted Hollis to teach the boy how to catch a baseball and teach him to use tools, but Hollis didn't have time for any of that.

⚫ ◆◆◆ ⚫

I drank a couple of cans of beer every night to give me a buzz and help me get to sleep. Auntie LaRue had told me that I didn't need to be drinking, but she wasn't going through what I was going through. But alas, she was right. I first admitted to myself that I was a functioning alcoholic. Then I poured the six-pack that I had just bought down the drain. And I never drank again. It had to be that drastic, because otherwise, how was I going to help Jewel get through treatment and continue to take care of the other kids?

The night before Jewel's first radiation treatment, I sent all the kids to bed early because I wanted to be alone to think. So many things were running through my mind, like when Jewel was little. She'd hated eating and would be late for school because I insisted that she eat her oatmeal or cereal.

I was thinking about Hodgkin's disease. How did my daughter get the disease anyway? I had asked the doctor that question, and he had given me what I felt was a completely unsatisfactory answer.

"I don't know," he'd said. "We don't know yet why people get Hodgkin's disease."

The doctor's response was only helpful in the sense that he hadn't said that I had caused her illness. Since the diagnosis, I had been wondering if I had done something to cause her illness. No one who I knew of in my family had ever had cancer, so I had no point of reference for Jewel's situation. Since I had no contact with the paternal side of Jewel's family, I didn't know if anyone in his family had had cancer.

I was sitting at the kitchen table, trying to eat some soup. I was feeling hopeless, sorry for myself and my kids. When the doorbell rang, I jumped because it startled me out of my musings. It wouldn't be Hollis at the door. He had a key. Anyway, he was out of town on his over-the-road truck driving job.

Wells's parents were going to come in the morning to take Jewel and me to her first radiation treatment. I moved the yellow curtain aside to look out the window.

Rosalie stood on the other side of the door!

I opened the door, she stepped in, and I fell into her arms. I was crying, and she was patting me on the back like a mother burping a baby.

We disengaged, and I said, "Rosalie, I didn't know you were coming to Buffalo."

"I know you didn't. That was the point. I wanted to surprise you."

"I just didn't know you cared that much."

"Of course I care. I know I'm a tough old broad, but I do have *some* feelings."

We both laughed.

"And I know I was mean to you and Viv sometimes when we were young, but everybody knows I didn't have a bit of sense back in the day."

"No, you didn't," I agreed, and we laughed some more.

The laugher felt good. And I was *so* glad to see my cousin. It's nice to have people who've known you for a lifetime. You don't have to pretend with them; you *can't* pretend.

We sat down over hot tea, and our conversation turned serious.

"Lilly, I'm so sorry about Vivian passing. You know I wanted to come for your housewarming, but I couldn't get the time off from work at the time. I wish I could have. I would have at least been able to see her one more time."

"I understand. I know you loved Viv. And I miss my sister."

"I have something for you. It's from Art and me to help you out with Jewel or whatever you need to use it for." She handed me an envelope containing $300.

Rosalie told me briefly about life in California with her husband and children. Then I updated her on Jewel's situation.

"This is rough, Lil. But I'm here to support you however I can."

"Thank you," I said.

Then I confided in her about Hollis. "I don't like or get along with him," I admitted. "Actually, I can't stand the sight of Hollis, and it's just adding to all the anxiety I have." I was relieved to divulge my secret to Rosalie.

I had told Hollis in the beginning that I didn't like him. All those months with him, I had been trying to engender good feelings that just wouldn't come.

"Wow," Rosalie said. "I wasn't expecting to hear this. I thought you two were in love."

"Hardly. I wish I'd never met Hollis Bowens. He does help me out financially, but he's such a childish man. He refuses to grow up. And I certainly don't need any more children to take care of. He's a party man. The more I think about it, the more I realize that he's far from being a family man."

"How is he with the kids?"

"He's been supportive about Jewel's illness, but he's more like a friend to them than a father. I want him to spend more time with Anthony. He makes promises but never gets around to it."

"Maybe it has something to do with Anthony being another man's son."

Rosalie's words slapped me in the face. "Maybe." I told her that I was grateful for Wells's father, Pops, spending time with my son.

"So what do you plan on doing about your situation with Hollis?"

"I don't know. I feel like I'm stuck. I'm living out here with sick kids, and I don't have a driver's license. I feel like I'm just stuck with him."

After a few seconds of silence, I told Rosalie to be thankful that she had a good, responsible husband. Rosalie didn't fulfill her lofty girlhood dream of becoming a track and field star, but she was living a good life.

"I *am* thankful for that. He is a very good father. Sometimes I think I don't deserve him. Anyway, Lil, it occurred to me that none of the sisters in Buffalo have a driver's license. Since you're probably the one in need of a license the most, why don't you learn how to drive?"

Good advice! Why *didn't* I have a license? I had a car that was sitting in my garage, waiting to be used. I *was* stuck—stuck in an old way of thinking and in feeling like a victim. Just like when I was a kid and

Rosalie's presence had stirred something in me, it happened again. The word *empowerment* came into my consciousness.

Rosalie stayed with us for five days, and we had a big dinner out at my house. Thankfully, she used her rental car to take Jewel to her radiation sessions for the rest of the week.

Jewel's radiation sessions were daily for nine weeks. I couldn't always make it to the treatments because I had to work. But friends and family helped us out by making sure Jewel got to the hospital, staying with her, and taking her back home. The Marconis from the earring store even helped out several times.

The first day of Jewel's treatment was a horror. We sat in a long hallway in the hospital's basement with lots of other people, each awaiting his or her turn. The wait seemed endless, and I felt like I was sitting in a dungeon. The hospital is now a totally modern, beautiful facility, but back then, it was uninviting.

The long wait was agonizing, and Jewel broke down crying. The only other time that I knew of her breaking under the weight of her circumstances was after the surgery when she was lying on a table under a scanning machine. She was screaming out for me in pain.

During that long wait, I comforted her as best I could. When her name was finally called, I was allowed to go into the room with her so the doctor and technician could explain how the treatment was administered. Once they were finished, I kissed Jewel on the forehead and had to return to the hall to wait.

Shortly after the treatments began, Jewel's curly black hair began falling out in the back of her head. She didn't seem fazed by her hair falling out; she just continued to style the rest of her hair as usual. She was usually nauseous and weak. One day, she fainted, hitting her head against the wall. The large curlers in her hair left a large hole in the wall. Her skin turned a dark crusty brown, and she could peel it off like you'd peel the skin off an orange. She endured all of it gracefully and remained strong and brave. She never complained and probably handled the whole ordeal better than I would have been able to.

Jewel had started the eighth grade at the beginning of the school year, but once she had the biopsy, she never returned to finish out the year. The school district provided her with a tutor. The teacher was a kind man who took his job seriously but made learning interesting by doing things like bringing a telescope to the house for Jewel and her siblings to look through in the backyard.

⸺ ◆◆◆ ⸺

With the grueling radiation treatment behind us, I had to turn my attention to my transportation dilemma. Everything had been so convenient to get to when we lived in the projects. If I couldn't get somewhere in ten or fifteen minutes by walking, I could hop on a bus. If the bus wasn't convenient, I could take a taxi. Downtown and my job were five minutes away in opposite directions, and the kids' school had been five minutes from my job.

Malone was a completely different story. Jewel was on the mend, but she had to go to the cancer hospital for frequent checkups, not to mention the needs of the other kids. And taking the bus to and from the city every day for work was grueling for me.

Taking the bus in Malone meant having to make the long walk from our house to the main highway. We had to cross the busy road and then wait for the bus, which ran on an infrequent schedule.

I talked to Hollis, and he agreed to teach me to drive. The lessons didn't go well at all.

"Pump the break. Pump the break, Lilly! Pull over and stop the car. What are you tryin' to do? Get us killed?"

"Stop yelling at me," I shot back at Hollis.

"Pull over. *Now.*"

I pulled over to the curb. Hollis and I switched places. When he got in the driver's side of his long red Ford, he took a deep breath, exhaled, and turned to look me straight in the face. "You can't be runnin' red lights. If you were takin' your driving test and you did that, you would automatically fail. You know what? You're never gonna pass that test, and I don't know why you picked the wintertime of all times to learn to drive. Why, of all times, did you decide *now to* learn to drive?"

I felt dumb, and I was defensive. "I should have learned a long time ago, but you know that I need to drive because we're living out here in the suburbs. I have too many responsibilities to have to depend on the bus."

It was my turn to take in a long breath and exhale. I made a quick decision. "You don't have to teach me anymore. I'm just gonna go to driving school. I'll just pay for my driving lessons."

I thought he was going to lighten up and tell me, "Look, baby, let's just calm down, and I'll teach you to drive." Instead, he said, "Well, you just do that because you ain't gone get me killed."

Hollis was a very good driver, the best in New York State, to hear him tell it. He had dropped out of high school in his senior year to join the air force. He had managed to earn a good living for himself once he was out of the service. After several years as a mechanic, he'd switched jobs and become an over-the-road truck driver.

Winter wasn't the greatest time to learn to drive, but I had no more time to waste, so I signed up for lessons. At least a paid instructor wouldn't be yelling at me! I drove over the curb my first time around taking the road test. Of course I failed. The next time around, I gave myself a good talking to in the bathroom mirror. I told myself to be calm and concentrate because failing was not an option.

I did pass the test the second time around. I got Wells's car registered, and on the first day that the roads were clear, the kids and I took my maiden voyage to Niagara Falls. I felt like a bird let go from captivity as I drove over the skyway. Al Green was in the eight-track player. I loved Al Green and once had a dream that I married him. When he crooned, "I am so in love with you," I replied, "And I'm so in love with you too!"

*** ✦✦✦ ***

There had been so many obstacles and hurdles in my life. But I began to take on a different perspective. I was viewing life in a more progressive mind-set. With that in mind, because Jewel's radiation treatments were over and I now had my driver's license and a car, I couldn't come up with any more reasons to stay with Hollis. So I did what I had promised myself I was going to do once Jewel had her final treatment.

I asked Hollis to leave.

He was taken aback. Shaking his head, he said, "I thought we were gettin' married."

"We're not, Hollis. I just want you to pack up your stuff and leave."

The relief I felt once he was in his car and backing out the driveway was only exceeded by the relief I felt when Jewel's treatments were over. I felt like I could finally begin to live the life I was meant to live.

I asked my mother to move out to the house with us.

"I can't," Mama said. "I got my own apartment. And I have to help out with Vivian's kids. But I can come out once in a while to help you out."

Mama did come out to stay for a few days at a time. She would plant a vegetable garden in the back of the house.

Hollis called me a couple of times, but I told him he needed to forget my number.

••• ◆◆◆ •••

Someone had told me about a job opening for an LPN at a county clinic south of the city and closer to my home. After inquiring about the position, I really wanted it.

The clinic's clientele were people from the small community. They ran the gamut, from infants needing immunization shots to teens needing physicals to play sports to the middle-aged and elderly trying to maintain a reasonable portion of health. I had learned about all those phases of life in nursing school.

The starting salary was decent, and the job offered good benefits, which included a pension. The hours were from 7:00 a.m. to 4:00 p.m. and no weekends, which pretty much coincided with the kids' school hours.

After being offered the job on the same day as the interview, I was thrilled to accept it.

Working at the clinic had another benefit for me. Gladys Jefferies was the longtime clinic receptionist. For some reason, she took an immediate liking to me. We had lunch together during my first week on the job.

I was flabbergasted when this soft-spoken woman, who was a minister's wife, confided in me that, when she was nineteen years old, she'd started walking the streets of the downtown red-light district as a prostitute. She said she had done that work for about a year.

We were sitting at the table in the small clinic lunchroom. Gladys laughed. "I know. You can't believe it, can you?"

I didn't respond because I didn't want to offend Gladys.

"I can't believe it either. And I tell you, it's only by the grace of God that I'm still here."

"How did you get out of that life?" I asked.

"A group of people from St. Luke Baptist Church used to come downtown and talk to me and the other girls who were working the streets. What I liked was that they didn't judge us. They genuinely made an effort to get to know us. They asked us if there was anything that they could do for us, and they invited us to church."

Gladys visited the church, and she said she loved it. They encouraged her to reunite with her family and go to school to get some training so she could get off the streets.

"I believe somebody was praying for me because I could have been killed, or any number of other things could have happened to me. But I got saved, and I eventually married a minister. The rest is history."

"How long ago was that?" I asked.

"That was over fifteen years ago."

I couldn't sleep the night of my lunch with Gladys. I had shared a little bit of my story with her, and she'd said, "Lilly, God loves you so much. Whatever's going on with you, you can turn it over to Jesus, and your life will be changed forever."

Gladys was straitlaced and normal. The fact that she was a former prostitute had a profound effect on me. Her situation turned my ideas about God upside down. She'd said, "You don't come to him perfect. You come to him just as you are, flaws and all."

I pulled out my Bible and opened it to the passage that Gladys had told me to read. She'd told me to pray as I read. The passage was in Corinthians, and it said, "Therefore, if any man be in Christ, he is a new creature: old things are passed away; behold, all things are become new."

Something happened to me as I sat in my bed reading that passage. If Jesus could save Gladys and bring change to her life, then there was hope for me. I had been walking through life feeling so badly about myself. I'd been beating myself up about the poor choices I had made about men. I felt bad about not fulfilling my desire to be a fashion designer. I despised myself for ever having gotten involved with Hollis. I pretty much felt like I had prostituted myself to keep myself and my kids safe.

But if God could save Gladys, he surely could save me. Sitting on my bed, I bowed my head and asked God to forgive me for my sins. I asked him to come into my life and help me to be a better person. Like Gladys said, *I got saved!*

••• ❖❖❖ •••

In the meantime, I was trying to make sense of my decision to move to Malone. Auntie LaRue told me that the Lord had blessed me with my new suburban home. Everyone had been so impressed with me having a home built. Much to my dismay, though, Malone wasn't the paradise I had thought it was going to be.

Malone was a peaceful, clean community. You couldn't find a piece of trash on the ground. The school system was rated near the top in the county. But for all the area had to offer, there was definitely no welcoming committee that showed up at our door with homemade cookies.

In fact, some of the people in our new town behaved as if they had never seen a black person before. Several times when the kids were walking down the road, someone would call out from a passing car, yelling at them to, "Go back to Africa." And they were called *jungle bunnies*.

As if that weren't bad enough, one night when the kids were in the living room watching television, they started yelling for me to come and look outside. There, on the front lawn, was a belated welcoming present in the form of a small burning cross. A kind stranger came along and doused the fire with a fire extinguisher. The man left without saying a word. I reported the incident to the police, but the perpetrator was never found.

It was crazy. Was I in the 1940s down south? Or was I in New York in the 1970s? None of those evil things were supposed to be happening. I honestly didn't know what to do, but I knew I wanted to move back to the city where all my friends and family lived.

"Mama, I'm movin'," I said. "I'm not stayin' out here. I'm packin' up our stuff, and we're leaving."

"Well, you can come and stay here for a while. But you know there's not that much room here for five extra people."

I couldn't walk away from my home. And we had as much right to live in Malone as anyone else.

••• ❖❖❖ •••

Gladys had told me that God loved me, *so much*. I was growing in my faith, but I still didn't understand the concept of *God's love*. As a woman who'd never known her biological father, I couldn't understand how a God who I could not see and who seemed so far away could love *me*. I heard someone say that God is closer than you think.

I took the kids to the beach. While they frolicked in the water, I sat on a blanket reading the Bible and quietly prayed. I was asking God to give me clarity. Actually, what I needed was for God to reveal himself to me.

I thought about all those messed-up relationships I'd had with men—so many heartaches, struggles and mistakes. All those men were fallible, and I was too. But according to the Bible, God is *not* fallible, and he *is* love.

I stopped reading and looked up to the blue sky. My mind went back to when I was a kid visiting Chicago, floating on my back and looking up at the sky. Thinking about God. Wondering about God and wanting to ask him some questions.

Now I had different questions. I wanted to know about relationship. People talk about religion, but I wasn't interested in that. I needed to know God for myself. I wanted to feel his presence.

I asked for what I needed. "Lord, please help me to know that you love me." I prayed for the faith to believe that he loved me as much as Gladys said he did.

I sensed that I was hearing the word *faith*.

I have since learned that everything a person gets from God is through faith.

As the years went by, I did come to realize that not only am I loved by him, but I am also very valuable. That changed everything for me, from how I think to how I treat others.

Growing spiritually helped me to understand a lot of what I'd gone through in my life and to put things into perspective. God always had his hand on my life, even when I wasn't thinking about him. He waited for me. And I learned that trials help you to grow, to mature, and to become empathetic.

Taking a spiritual growth journey is the wisest thing I've ever done in my life!

CHAPTER 13

❖❖❖

IN 1984, FOR my forty-fifth birthday, my kids and friends surprised me with a birthday party—my first ever. The party was held at Gladys's house. She wasted no time in introducing me to a friend from church, Canton Kennedy. I remembered seeing him when I visited Gladys's church one Sunday. He was a slender man, no more than a couple of inches taller than me, and he was nice-looking and a smooth operator. Instead of shaking my hand, he kissed it. I maintained a cool exterior, but I swooned on the inside.

"Happy birthday, Ms. McClendon," he said.

"Thank you."

Gladys had made herself scarce after our introduction. His light brown face was completely free of any facial hair, and he had a light in his hazel eyes that made it hard for me to look away. His smile showed perfect white teeth. It was a hot evening, and he wore a short-sleeved shirt that showed muscular arms. He was perfect.

I picked up right away that he was a very confident man. I was right, because he had known me all of five minutes when he asked if he could call me sometime.

"Uh. Uh. I don't know."

"I'm sorry," Canton said. "Forgive me for putting you on the spot like that. I guess I just got caught up in the moment of meeting such a lovely lady."

I laughed, not knowing what to say to such a forward, although not off-putting man. I glanced around the house at the happy scene. Gladys's dining room table was set with an assortment of finger foods and wine and soda. In a corner of the room were wrapped presents. The sounds of smooth jazz filled the room.

"This is very nice," I said. "They did a good job of surprising me. I had no idea about the party."

"Excuse me everyone," Gladys said, rescuing me from my awkwardness. "If you could all gather in the dining room for a moment."

When we did so, Gladys said, "If everyone will take a drink from the table, I want to give a toast to the birthday girl."

Everyone raised his or her glass.

Gladys said, "I just want to first thank God for my precious friend, Lilly McClendon." Gladys turned to me. "Lilly, I am a better person for having you in my life. You are the personification of perseverance. And you are greatly loved. Here's to many more happy and healthy years."

"Happy birthday," everyone sang out.

Since it was a special occasion, I decided to do something daring by giving Canton my phone number. Of course I never would have done it had he not been Gladys's friend. He was a policeman and owned rental property in the city. He attended the same church as Gladys. The church's men's group mentored boys and young men who were at risk for taking a wrong turn in life, and he was part of that group.

Again Canton wasted no time. He called me after the party and asked me out on a date. I said yes to the date and lay in bed after talking to him, musing about every unexpected minute, from the party itself to meeting Canton Kennedy. How was a woman who hadn't been on a date in well over a decade supposed to behave on a first date?

I realized in my musings that I missed the everyday presence of a man's voice in my life. I had a full, busy life with work, family, friends and church, but I missed male companionship.

"Mom, you should meet a nice man who you can spend time with." That was Jewel, and she had strongly suggested that more than once.

I had gone out on a couple of dates since ending my relationship with Hollis. When I found out that he had a girlfriend, I told the man goodbye. After that, I had suppressed any needs or desires. But once I met Canton, I felt as though I had been lying to myself all those years.

For the first time in my life, I was in a good place mentally. I was no longer anxious. I was happy and healthy and didn't have young children to be concerned about. Yes, I was ready for a relationship, at least a friendship.

Still, I was nervous about going out with Canton. I had lunch with Gladys the afternoon before the date, and I reminded her that I hadn't been on a date in years.

"Lilly, you're a wonderful person. Just be yourself," she advised. "You have a lot to talk about. And you can see that Canton's a great guy, so just enjoy yourself."

The year before I met Canton, I had sold my house in Malone and bought a house in the city. Regina, who was sick more than she was well, from the sickle cell disease, still lived with me.

"You look great," Canton said as he stepped into my foyer.

"Thank you."

I wore my favorite orange summer dress, and I had taken care with my hair and makeup. I was pleased with the results.

Canton was a perfect gentleman. While we waited for our meal at one of Buffalo's best restaurants, Canton said, "When I was around thirteen, sittin' on the porch doing my homework, a woman passed by our house, and I whistled at her. What I didn't know was that my father was standing in the doorway. Dad promised me that if I ever disrespected a woman like that again, it would be an immensely bad day for me."

We both laughed.

Canton's father had demonstrated how to treat a woman by loving his mother. When his parents quarreled, they did it in private. When he got home from work, Canton's father would sneak up behind his wife and wrap her in a bear hug. He would kiss her and tell her he loved her. He was tough on the boys, but he loved them and would plant a kiss on the boys' forehead when the mood struck him.

"I never knew my father," I said. "He was killed on the railroad tracks down south. I was a little girl when that happened. And then, when my husband died, I was so despondent I contemplated killing myself. I was sorry for him and sorry for myself. Most of all, I was sorry for my kids because they wouldn't have their father."

"I'm sorry," Canton said.

Canton had been divorced for over ten years. He'd had primary custody of his two boys, who were in their early twenties when Canton and I met.

"She didn't love me no more," he said lightly. "I can joke about it now, but at the time, it wasn't so funny. I've been single ever since. I dated a few times, but nothing serious. I never thought I would meet the right woman, until I met you."

"This *is* just a first date. You might find that you don't like me."

"I doubt that, Lilly McClendon."

⚫ ◆◆◆ ⚫

I liked Canton. A lot. My kids liked him too. We began spending more time together. But it took a while for me to feel comfortable enough to visit him at his house. His house was beautiful. My favorite part was the enclosed porch that was heated in the winter and cool in the summer.

"You're not very trusting of men, are you?" Canton asked me one cool fall evening as we were driving to his house in North Buffalo. I had finally agreed to go to his house for a pasta dinner.

"Is that funny?" I asked because he was laughing.

"No, but it's very obvious." He patted my hand. "Relax. It's just dinner. You're as safe with me as you would be with a newborn baby."

"Okay," I said. I did believe him because we had been dating for a couple of months and nothing strange had happened during that time. After dinner that evening, we sat on the loveseat in his sunroom. Canton put his arm around my shoulders and leaned in to kiss me. It was a gentle kiss on the lips, and then after he lingered with a kiss on my forehead he told me he had to take me home before we got something started. "I don't want to corrupt your morals," he joked.

⚫ ◆◆◆ ⚫

It was the summer of 1985 and nearly a year had gone by since Canton and I had met. After those first halting dates, Canton and I had practically become inseparable. One afternoon, we spontaneously decided to go to the beach. We sat by the shore, watching the waves crashing against the shore. My sandals were off, and I was digging my feet in the sand.

From the time I was a child, I'd loved the beach. The water and sky seemed to meet with a kiss. Sometimes the water would be angry and the sky brooding. No matter if it was a beach or a lake or Niagara Falls, I was drawn to the water. Water seemed to wash over my soul, cleansing it and bringing clarity. So it seemed apropos that Canton would propose to me at the beach.

"We're not getting any younger," Canton said.

"This is true."

He pulled a large white-and-rose-gold ring out of his pocket. "Lilly, will you marry me? I know the beach on a Saturday afternoon is not the most romantic place to ask you, but I would love for you to be my wife."

I looked from the ring to the smiling man who was poised to put it on my finger. Of course, it was plenty romantic. "Yes. Yes, I'll marry you, Canton."

So we were engaged and planning to have a romantic Valentine's Day wedding.

••• ❖❖❖ •••

A couple of weeks later, we had taken our grandkids to the park. We tossed a Nerf football with the kids and pushed them on the swings, and then we had a picnic lunch. Afterward, we went to Canton's to watch a movie on his enclosed porch, which was something we all loved to do.

The movie had barely started when we heard someone pounding on the front door. Canton and I looked at each other. The doorbell worked, so there was no need to bang on the door.

"You stay here with the kids. I'll see who that is," Canton said.

I heard Jewel's voice, and she sounded like she was in agony.

"What's wrong, Grandma?" Jewel's little boy asked.

"It's okay, honey. You kids stay here and watch the movie. I'll be right back." I knew I wouldn't be right back. I went into the living room with a sense of dread coursing through my veins.

Jewel was with her husband, who had a pained look on his face.

"Mom," Jewel said as she fell into my arms.

I didn't want to know what the matter was. Jewel was like me. We saved our high emotions for really serious matters.

"Mama, Regina's dead. She had a crisis, and they say she had a heart attack and died. We have to go to the hospital."

Canton made arrangements for his neighbor to watch the kids while the four of us adults went to the hospital. When we got there, I ran through the emergency rooms doors, stopped at the nurse's station, told them who I was, and demanded to see my child.

It was the saddest sight a mother could ever see. Regina lay lifeless on the bed. Her eyes were closed, but she looked as if she were only sleeping. We all walked into the room, and the doctor came in behind us. The only thing I remember him saying was for us to take all the time we needed.

"Oh God, help me," I cried as I ran my hand along the side of her face.

Regina had larger hands than normal for a woman, hands like her father's. I put my hands in hers. I caressed her hands and looked to make sure her chest wasn't moving up and down. It wasn't.

"She's gone," I said. If I said it out loud, I had to accept it.

My daughter had defied the odds by living well past her fourteenth birthday. She had lived with sickle cell crises, but she'd basically lived her life around the pain. She had graduated from community college and worked part-time as a medical secretary in a doctor's office. She did her best. I'll always remember how perfectly that late-summer day started out and how tragically it ended.

⚬⚬ ❖❖❖ ⚬⚬

Two days after the funeral, I took a long walk in the park. As I walked, I thought about Regina. She had loved life, and she had been funny. She had done her best in spite of her illness. She was always thinking about me. She would buy me little gifts and bring me flowers. "They say bring the flowers to the living," she had said one day.

When I got back home from my walk, I called Canton and told him that I couldn't marry him.

"Why?" he asked.

"Because things have changed," I told him. "I've changed my mind. I would just rather be alone."

"That's your grief talking." There was a long pause. Then he said, "Is this really a conversation that we should be having over the phone?"

Canton insisted on coming to my house to talk. I told him that he was wasting his time because my mind was made up. "I'm *not* getting married," I insisted.

But he came anyway.

When Canton arrived at the house, he stepped into the kitchen, shrugged off his jacket and asked, "What's going to be different with you in six months?" Canton was a gentle man, but he was very direct.

"What do you mean what's going to be different in six months?"

Canton laid his jacket over a kitchen chair and sat beside me. I was stirring honey in a cup of tea.

"I mean, after the grief of losing Regina becomes bearable, do you think you'll want to get on with your life as it was? Or do you think you'll want to be alone for the rest of your life?"

Canton wiped my tears with his hand. He asked softly, "Lilly, can you see me in your future?" His face was so close to mine that I could smell the peppermint gum he was chewing. "Do you see me in your future?" he asked.

"I don't know."

"Okay. Let me ask you this. What do you think Regina would want you to do? Do you think she would want you to change your plans because of her passing? Or do you think she would want you to marry the man you love?"

He put his hand to my chin and lifted my face so that I looked into his eyes. They were moist with tears. "Regina was a wonderful girl, and I wish I could bring her back, but I can't. What I can do is be with you. You can cry on my shoulder. You can scream at me. You can even throw things at me, as long as they're little things and you don't throw too hard." He smiled, and I smiled, in spite of my agony.

I didn't know what I'd done to deserve Canton Kennedy. I didn't have to fight for his love. I didn't have to fight with him or wonder when he was going to take his love away. He was easy to love and hard to say no to.

I sighed and said, "Regina would want us to get married. I love you, Canton, and I want to marry you."

⚬⚬ ✦✦✦ ⚬⚬

The father in heaven had saved the best for last. We did get married on Valentine's Day. Ever since I'd learned about Hawaii in high school, I had promised myself I was going to make it there someday. It had always seemed little more than a pipe dream. When Canton and I took a honeymoon trip to Waikiki, the beauty and serenity were a balm for my wounded soul after losing Regina.

Canton was a good man, and we would have a lot of good years together before he would die from pneumonia a few years before this writing.

⸺ ◆◆◆ ⸺

It's now 2018. I'm seventy-eight years old and taking a panoramic view of life in my mind's eye. I can say that it's been quite a journey. I have great-grandchildren now.

When Regina died, I didn't think I would ever get over it. Of course I think about her every day, but time has eased the pain.

Anthony, who had gotten in with the wrong crowd for a while, came back to his senses and took an apprenticeship program for carpentry. He married and had two girls and a boy.

Bridgett moved to North Carolina in the early '80s. She took a job at the phone company and is living a good life. I always wanted her to get married and have kids. "When the right man comes along, I will," she'd say. I'm still waiting!

Jewel was declared to be in remission from cancer in summer 1974. When she was sixteen, she took her first plane ride, and it was to visit our relatives in Los Angeles. She stayed with Rosalie. I was happy for her to take the trip because she had been through so much.

She went to Disneyland, Knox Berry Farm, and the taping of a couple of sitcoms and met stars. She went horseback riding, and she became pretty good at crocheting, the craft I had learned as a teenager. As an adult, she experienced breast cancer twice, with the second diagnosis resulting in a double mastectomy. Studies have shown that survivors of childhood cancers have a higher risk than does the general population of being diagnosed with other cancers.

Jewel is a fighter, and thank God she is doing well. All my aunts and their spouses have passed on. I miss them. I think of my grandparents often.

Most of all, I miss my mother. She suffered a massive stroke, lingered on in the hospital for weeks, and then died. I was glad that Mama was around long enough to see me happily married. She enjoyed Canton's company. He was sweet to her, generous and kind.

Sometimes I sit at the kitchen table with my old photographs and I get misty-eyed. Reminiscing tends to stir up the emotions.

After working at the clinic for more than twenty years, I retired. Canton helped me secure a small store in a strip mall. I turned it into a gift shop where I sold novelty items and some clothing that I made (shirts and dresses). It kept me busy. I actually couldn't believe my good fortune. I had finally realized my long-ago dream of earning a living by making things that I sold. I didn't get rich, but I didn't need to. The satisfaction of realizing my long-held dream was more than enough for me.

Gladys had also retired from the clinic, and she passed away some years later. She had been my mentor, and I made sure to show her how much I appreciated her. *And* she had introduced me to Canton, so I was doubly grateful to her.

It's a strange thing getting old. So much has gone before you, and you're not quite sure of what the future holds. One thing is sure, though; you have more days behind than before you.

Times have changed. People are freer in their self-expression, like rainbow-colored hair and tattooed necks and arms and legs.

Life is drastically different from when I was a little girl in the backwoods of Georgia. We lived in lack for years, but it's the total opposite now. I've been blessed. I'm always giving things away because I have more than I need.

The technological advances are enough to make one's head spin. Jewel took a typing class in high school, and her teacher had some insight into the future. The teacher told the class that people would be able to talk on the phone and see each other as they carried on their conversation, à la FaceTime!

When I moved to Buffalo as a teen, the city had a population over five hundred thousand. But like many other Rust Belt towns, Buffalo experienced a downturn in the economy and a drastic decrease in population. Ironically, many blacks have moved back down south. But the city is experiencing a renaissance. I have come to love the place where I was forced to come to all those years ago.

Of course, nothing's perfect. Social unrest is everywhere, and segregation is a problem even today. We've made many advances, but we have so much further to go.

And these are dark times too.

So I pray.

9 781532 050893